"I Know You."

The man's voice held a challenge. Diamond looked up at him. Young, in his midtwenties, and full of himself. He stood with one hip cocked, his hand hanging loosely by his gun. On his face was an arrogant sneer, the kind Diamond used to like to wipe off faces in his younger days. "Do you?"

"I'm better than you!" he said. "With a gun, I mean."

"Fine," Diamond said, and looked back down at his beer.

The man looked around, grinning at his two friends standing at the bar. "So what do you intend to do about it?"

"Nothing."

"Everybody here will think you're yeller."

"So what? I don't care what they think," Diamond said, "and I don't care what you think."

"What's going on?"

The young man turned at the sound of the voice and saw Clint Adams standing there.

Diamond looked at Clint and said, "It strikes me that if I tell this youngster who *you* are, he may decide to leave me alone and try for you."

Also in THE GUNSMITH series

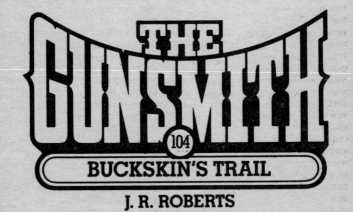

THE GUNSMITH

104

BUCKSKIN'S TRAIL

J. R. ROBERTS

JOVE BOOKS, NEW YORK

BUCKSKIN'S TRAIL

A Jove Book/published by arrangement with
the author

PRINTING HISTORY
Jove edition/August 1990

ISBN: 0-515-10387-X

Jove Books are published by The Berkley Publishing Group,
200 Madison Avenue, New York, New York 10016.
The name "Jove" and the "J" logo
are trademarks belonging to Jove Publications, Inc.

PRINTED IN THE UNITED STATES OF AMERICA

10 9 8 7 6 5 4 3 2 1

PROLOGUE

Buckskin Frank Leslie was a small, wiry man who carried twin Colt Peacemakers on his hips. Leslie wore his hair long and flowing, with a mustache to match, and was constantly clad in buckskins, which is why he had come to be called Buckskin Frank Leslie.

For the past three years Leslie had been half owner of a saloon in Brightwater, Arizona. His partner in the saloon was a man named Clint Adams, otherwise known as the Gunsmith. Almost four years before, Adams had come to town just in time to side with Leslie in a fight to keep his saloon.* In the process, Adams had bought into the saloon, and since that time Leslie had been sending a share of the profits to Adams's bank in Labyrinth, Texas.

He had not seen Clint Adams since then, although

*THE GUNSMITH #16

1

they had communicated from time to time by telegraph.

When Leslie had first bought the saloon it had been in an attempt to settle down. Never could Leslie have imagined that he would stay settled down for nearly four years. Of late, however, he'd been getting fed up with owning a bar—and *tending* it, most of the time—and he was thinking of moving on.

He was thinking about it now, even though he was in bed with a lovely blond girl named Joy Darling. Clint Adams had hired Joy when she first came to town, and Leslie knew that Adams had often slept with the girl. After the Gunsmith left, however, Leslie and Joy had drifted into a comfortable arrangement, one that had them sharing a bed more often than not.

Joy rolled over as the morning sun drifted in through the window, and Leslie stared down at her large, rounded breasts. When they'd first met her breasts had been too big for her slender frame, but over the past three years she had filled out in other places and become a statuesque woman. Leslie always teased her about having finally grown into those fine tits.

He leaned over now and nibbled on her right nipple. She moaned, stretching her hands up over her head, and then she brought them down to cup his head as he sucked on the left nipple.

"Good morning," she said.

"Morning." His reply was muffled because he had worked his way down her body and was now face down between her legs. He let his tongue tease her for a few moments, knowing that it didn't take much to build her towards a climax. When his tongue flicked at her clitoris, she cried out to him.

"Bastard!" she said. "Tease! Oooh, come on, come on . . ."

He rose over her and slid into her, enjoying the way her steaming pussy surrounded him and sucked him in. When he was inside of her, he slid his hands beneath her to cup her buttocks, and he squeezed them tightly as he drove himself into her.

It was what they both referred to as a "waker-upper."

"About what we talked about last night . . ." he said.

She looked at him, and he could see the fear in her eyes.

"Yes?"

He hesitated, then said, "I've got to go, Joy."

"Frank . . ."

"I've thought about it a long time," he said. "I'm going to sign the saloon over to you. You'll be partners with Clint now."

She opened her mouth to protest but then thought better of it. She had always known that Frank Leslie would leave her some day, the same way Clint Adams had left. Neither of them was a man you could hold onto for very long. She told herself to be grateful that she and Frank had had three years together.

Now it was time for him to move on.

"Are you going to send a telegram to Clint?"

"Clint," he said, snorting. "My 'friend.' You'd

think he'd drop back here once or twice over these past three years. All those newspaper accounts we've read. While I've been settled down here, he's been out making a bigger name for himself.''

"You know he doesn't want—''

"Doesn't want the reputation?'' Leslie said. "A man who doesn't want a reputation doesn't show up in the papers so often, Joy.''

"Frank—''

"You know, if I'd been out there on the trail these past three years, I'd be a bigger name than he ever was!'' Leslie said, with a vehemence that startled her.

"Oh, Frank, no—''

"Probably bigger than Hickok.''

"Frank, I don't like hearing you talk like this.''

"I feel like breakfast,'' he said. He leaned over, kissed her, and slapped her on the rump. "Why don't you go down and order for us, huh?''

"Sure, Frank,'' she said. She stood up and began to dress. "When will you be leaving?'' she asked, without looking at him.

"End of the week, Joy,'' he said. "I'll have the papers drawn up to transfer the saloon to your name.''

"Sure, Frank,'' she said again. "I'll see you downstairs.''

After Joy Darling had left, Buckskin Frank Leslie stood up and walked naked to the window. He looked down at Brightwater's main street. This town had become a prison to him, and he was going to break out.

He was going to break out in more ways than one. He was going to hit the trail and become Buckskin Frank Leslie again, a man once feared for his prowess with a gun in either hand.

He would become a bigger name than his "friend" Clint Adams, the Gunsmith, could ever hope to be.

Buckskin Frank Leslie was out of the saloon business, and back into the business he was born to.

Guns.

ONE

Clint Adams walked down the main street of Labyrinth, Texas, exchanging greetings with the men and women of the town. He knew they knew who he was, and he knew that many of them simply greeted him because of who he was, the Gunsmith. When a man had a reputation with a gun he was usually treated well by the townspeople—most of the time out of fear.

Clint didn't like thinking that a lot of these people feared him, but he had learned to live with it. A few of them knew him personally on one level or another, however, and their greetings were genuine.

The only man in town who knew him very well was his friend, Rick Hartman, the owner of Rick's Place, the largest saloon in town. T.C., Rick's black bartender, probably knew him better than anyone else in town except Rick, but it could not be said that T.C. knew him well.

Clint had been in Labyrinth two weeks this visit, and was starting to get itchy to move again.

It was late afternoon, and Clint was on his way to dinner. After dinner he would go to Rick's, have a few beers, play some poker, and then go back to his hotel. There was always an excellent chance that he would not go back to his room alone. The turnover of girls at Rick's was like that of any saloon. Women came and went often, but Rick usually only hired those who were sure to bring in business with their looks. Very often Clint brought one of them back to his room with him. Rick usually picked out a girl and stuck with her for a few months, sometimes until she left. Rick's girl this month was a fiery redhead—fiery in *both* senses of the word. If Rick hadn't gotten to her first, Clint would have been only too happy to try and help her quench her fire.

He entered Gap's Restaurant and took a small table against the wall. Gap was the owner of the place, as well as the cook, and he made the best coffee Clint had ever tasted. Gap had only been in business in Labyrinth about six months, but Clint had become a regular customer whenever he was in town.

Clint had noticed something about Gap. He had as large a turnover in waitresses as Rick had in saloon girls, but Gap didn't have anything near Rick's taste in women. Invariably, Gap hired homely women, and he was usually sleeping with one of them. When Clint had asked Gap about it, the man had smiled his gap-toothed smile and said,

"When they're homely, who cares when they leave ya?"

These days Gap had only one waitress, so he had to wait on tables himself from time to time. When he saw Clint enter, Gap walked right over to him.

"Coffee to start?" he asked.

"You know it."

"Comin' up."

Gap was in his fifties, big and broad, and he carried a paunch around with him. His gap-toothed smile, from which he'd apparently gotten his name, had been his since he was sixteen, when he lost some teeth in a fight. "Over a gal, naturally—and she was worth it!"

Gap was a ladies' man, though Clint couldn't quite understand it. There was something about the big man that just drew women like flies—but they were usually homely.

"We make a good match," he often said, good-naturedly.

Gap's waitress this month was not nearly so homely as the others had been. Still, the nicest thing Clint could say about her was that she was "plain." She had red hair, like Rick's girl, though it was not red like fire but a deeper, burnished red. She also had freckles on her plain face. She had her back to Clint at the moment, and he noticed that she had a broad, if firm, ass. When she turned and smiled at him, he realized that she actually had a nice smile and a nice set of breasts.

When Gap returned with a full pot of coffee, Clint said, "Your taste in women is changing, Gap."

"I know it," Gap said, "but she was the best I could do. Too good lookin', huh?"

"Well," Clint said, "let's say she's not nearly what I'm used to. What's her name?"

"Brianne."

"What?"

Gap repeated it.

"That's a nice name."

"I know it. Irish, I think."

Clint reflected on her freckled face and red hair and said, "I'm sure it is."

"Want to try her out, Clint?" Gap asked. "A man always shares with his friends, you know."

Clint laughed and said, "I think I'll settle for one of your special steak dinners, Gap."

"Comin' up."

Clint watched Brianne wait on some customers while he waited on his steak. She had a nice, economical way of moving—not a motion was wasted—and her hair moved nicely on her shoulders. Clint had slept with a lot of women over the years, most of them beautiful, some of them less than beautiful—pretty, some plain, one or two who could have been called homely, one who could even be called fat—but there was always something nice about them. The way they felt, the way they smelled, the way they moved. All women, he thought, had something to recommend them, even the homeliest.

He loved women, plain and simple, in all shapes and sizes, and Brianne was a woman, for sure.

Briefly, he considered Gap's offer. She would

never have qualified for a job at Rick's, but he had a feeling she would be no disappointment in bed.

She turned at one point and caught him looking at her. She cocked her head at him and smiled, then walked over to his table.

"You're Clint Adams."

"I am."

"I've seen you in here once before. I been here a week."

He frowned. He hadn't noticed her that first time. He wondered why.

"Can I get you something while you're waiting for your dinner?" she asked.

"Uh, a newspaper might be nice, if you have one."

"Sure, I'll get it."

She went to a corner of the room and picked up a paper from an empty table.

"Somebody left it," she said, handing the paper to him.

He noticed that it was not a copy of the *Labyrinth Banner* but the *Tylerville Gazette*. He knew that Tylerville was a small town in western Texas that was growing by leaps and bounds. Apparently they had themselves a bonafide newspaper, which was roughly the same size as the *Banner*.

"Thanks, Brianne."

"Surely. I'll go and see if Gap has your dinner ready."

He nodded and watched her walk to the kitchen. Her ass was too broad for the rest of her, but that could be forgiven in someone as obviously good-natured as she was.

Clint shifted his attention to the front page of the paper and was stunned by the first headline he saw. Though not the largest headline, and further down the page, it jumped out at him because of the familiarity of the name.

"BUCKSKIN FRANK LESLIE DEAD" it said in bold type.

He read the article hastily, then slowed himself down and read it again. According to the story, Leslie had been gunned down somewhere in New Mexico. Apparently, the *Gazette*'s quality of reporting still left something to be desired. He read the article again and still did not know much beyond the fact that his friend Buckskin Frank Leslie was supposed to be dead.

"Bad news?"

He looked up and saw Gap standing there, holding his dinner.

"Yes," Clint said, "about a friend."

"Still want this?" Gap asked. "You don't look much like someone who wants to eat."

"No," Clint said, "I seem to have lost my appetite. Can you keep it warm?"

"Don't worry about it," Gap said. "If you come back I'll cook you up a fresh one. You go and do what you gotta do."

"Thanks, Gap," Clint said, standing up. "I'm going to do just that."

TWO

When Clint left Gap's he went directly to the telegraph office. During the walk he had composed his message, and he wrote it quickly for the clerk.

"I want to know as soon as an answer comes in," he told the man.

"Yessir. Will that be all?"

"I have another," Clint said. It had come to him in a flash.

The first telegram had gone to Tylerville, addressed to the editor of that town's paper, whose name, C.Z. White, he had taken from the copy he still held. Clint had requested as much information on the death of Frank Leslie as the *Tylerville Gazette* had.

The second telegram went to Brightwater, Arizona, the last place Clint had seen Buckskin Frank Leslie alive. Clint had not been in Brightwater for some time, but his profits from the saloon he owned with Leslie had come in like clockwork, deposited in his account in the Bank of Labyrinth.

If Frank Leslie had left Brightwater, Arizona, how come Clint didn't know about it?

He addressed the second telegram to Frank Leslie, hoping that the story in the *Gazette* would turn out to be bogus.

"I want to know as soon as an answer comes in on any one of these."

"Yessir."

Clint left the telegraph office, debating whether or not he should go back to Gap's. He decided that he still had no appetite, so he would go to Rick's for a drink and a talk.

It was an oddity that Labyrinth, Texas, had become the closest thing Clint Adams had to a home. He had been in Labyrinth when he heard of his friend Wild Bill Hickok's death. Hickok had been shot in the back of the head by a coward, and Clint had reacted to the news by falling into a bottle. It was Rick Hartman who had fished him out of that bottle. Since that time, whenever Clint wasn't traveling, he was in Labyrinth.

Now he had heard about the death of another friend and—as was the case with Hickok—he wanted to find out all he could about it.

He wasn't going to get drunk, though. Not this time.

He still wanted to talk to Rick, though.

That much had not changed.

THREE

Clint entered Rick's Place and went directly to the bar.

"Beer?" T.C. asked.

"Yeah."

"Kind of early tonight, ain't you?"

"Yeah."

T.C. gave him his beer. Frowning, he asked, "Something wrong?"

The black man was reading the look on his face, so Clint gave him the paper to read.

"Frank Leslie," T.C. said after a moment. "He's a friend of yours, ain't he?"

"Yes."

"I'm sorry to hear—"

"Don't be sorry yet, T.C.," Clint said. "I'm not accepting this as the truth—not yet."

"Checking it out?"

"I've sent two telegrams."

T.C. put the paper down on the bar. "Well then, I hope you find out it *ain't* true."

"Thanks."

"Want me to get the boss?"

Clint looked at the clock and saw that it was almost six.

"No, he'll be down soon anyway. Just send me another beer when this one is empty."

"You got it."

Clint went to a table in the back that he liked to use when he was in town. He was the only person who had a table, other than Rick himself.

As he sat down, Nancy came over. She was a small, brunette bundle of energy in her twenties who gave him hell in bed. It was all he could do to keep up with her. She was buxom and just shy of plump, with an infectious smile that displayed dimples.

"Hi," she said, sitting down.

"Hi."

"Ooh," she said, "that's not the same man I spent the night with."

"I'm sorry," he said, touching her hand. "I'm really not very good company now."

"Something happen?"

"Maybe," he said. "A friend of mine may be dead."

"Oh, I'm sorry."

"I'm checking into it, and I'd just as soon wait for the news alone, if you don't mind."

"Of course not, Clint," she said, standing up. "You just tell me when you change your mind, all right?"

He took her hand and kissed it.

"Thanks, honey."

As she walked away from the table, Nancy intercepted Sybil, a tall blonde. It was no secret among the girls that Clint had been to bed with more than one of them, and they all accepted that. *They* were friends, and *he* was their friend, so no one got possessive about the situation.

At six-fifteen, Rick Hartman came down the stairs with his redhead, Kelly. Kelly was about six inches taller than Rick in her heels, but that didn't bother either one of them. Rick's physical stature had nothing whatsoever to do with the kind of man he was. In many, many ways, he was the biggest man Clint knew.

When Rick saw Clint, he said something to Kelly, kissed her, and then walked over to the Gunsmith.

"You're in before me tonight," he said. "Uncontrollable thirst?"

Clint had his second beer in front of him, half full, and in response to Rick's words he pushed it away.

"Have a seat," Clint said.

Rick sat down, frowning, and Clint handed him the newspaper.

"What's this? The *Tylerville Gazette*? Where did you get this?"

"Over at Gap's," Clint said. "A customer left it behind. Look halfway down the page."

Rick did as Clint asked and his eyebrows went up.

"Leslie's dead?"

"If we're to believe this story. They have no particulars or facts to back it up."

"Have you checked?"

"I'm waiting for an answer now. What do you know about it?"

Rick Hartman had a remarkable communications system of his own all across the country. He got news in from all over and usually knew everything about every *thing* and every *one*.

"Nothing," he said now.

"Did you hear anything about him leaving Brightwater?"

"Not a thing," Rick said. "Did he?"

"I'm checking that out, too."

"Jesus, if he did and I didn't hear about it, I'm going to have to get my ears checked." Clint knew he wasn't really talking about the ears on his head but the "ears" that he had stretched across the country.

"I don't get it," Clint said. "If he did leave Brightwater, why didn't he let me know?"

"Face it, Clint," Rick said. "You and he haven't exactly been keeping in touch."

Clint stared at Rick for a moment, before replying. "It's hard for a man to keep in touch with *all* his friends."

"Hey, I know that," Rick said.

"You think he might have been upset that I haven't been to Brightwater?"

"I don't know," Rick said. "You know the man, not me. What do you think?"

Clint thought about it and shook his head, then thought again. "I'm not sure."

He wondered if any of the girls he'd known still worked at the Buckskin saloon. He wondered if Joy

Darling still worked for Frank—for *them*—or if Marlene Jory or Jesse Wells still lived there. Maybe he should have addressed his telegram to one of them—or all of them, since he had no way of knowing who was still there and who wasn't.

He picked up his beer and sipped it carefully. He could feel Rick's eyes on him.

"Don't worry," Clint said to him, knowing what he was thinking, "this is not the same thing."

"I didn't say a word."

"You don't have to."

Rick turned around and waved to one of the girls, Nancy, who brought him a beer. Sybil and Kelly were working the room, which was beginning to fill up. The covers had come off the gambling tables, and the action was starting to heat up.

"You know," Rick said, "I've been thinking about opening a bigger place."

"Where?" Clint asked, absently.

"San Francisco."

Clint had begun to lift his beer to his mouth, but he stopped when Rick's words hit him.

"Where?"

"San Francisco."

"When did you start thinking about this?"

"I've always thought about it, Clint," Rick said. "How could I be in this business and not fantasize about owning a place in Frisco?"

"People who live there don't call it that," Clint pointed out.

"I don't live there . . . yet."

"Have you ever been there?"

"Once or twice, years ago. I vowed to myself never to go back until I was ready."

"And you're ready?"

"Just about," he said. "I've got enough money to buy a place, but I don't know if I've got enough to buy a big enough place."

"What will you do with this place?"

"I don't know," Rick said, sitting back. "Sell it, I guess. You wouldn't be interested in buying it, would you?"

"What would I do with it? I'm never here."

"Let T.C. run it for you."

"You're not taking him with you?"

Rick shrugged. "I guess that'd be up to him. What about San Francisco?"

"What about it?"

"Want to be a partner? I could do it a lot sooner with a partner—a partner I could trust."

Clint hesitated, then looked at the newspaper on the table.

"Let me find out what's happened to my present partner before I give you an answer on that."

FOUR

After he had finished his beer, Rick Hartman moved to his own table, leaving Clint Adams alone with his thoughts. Several men approached Clint about a poker game, but he waved them away. When he called for a deck of cards, Sybil brought them and offered to sit, but he told her the same thing he had told Nancy, kissed her hand, and sent her off to work. After that he sat there playing solitaire, nursing a third beer that had been brought to him by Kelly.

There was another girl who worked in the saloon, a raven-black-haired girl named Carrie, but he had not seen her yet.

When the batwing doors opened at seven, Clint saw the clerk from the telegraph office. The man looked around, located Clint, and walked to his table.

"Got one answer for you, Mr. Adams."

"From where?"

"Tylerville."

Clint tipped the man and said, "Thank you."

The man wasn't out of the saloon before Clint began reading.

> CLINT ADAMS
>   NO FURTHER INFORMATION ON DEATH OF BUCKSKIN FRANK LESLIE. SORRY
>
>   C.Z. WHITE

"What the fuck!" Clint said, crumbling the telegram in his hand. If they had no information, why print the damned story?

Clint decided that one of the things he would have to do was pay a personal visit to C.Z. White.

Clint saw Rick looking over at him and shook his head slowly.

He resumed his solitaire playing.

At about eight o'clock, the clerk came into the saloon again.

"Brightwater," he said, handing Clint the flimsy.

"Thanks," Clint said, tipping him again.

The telegram was from Joy Darling.

> CLINT ADAMS
>   FRANK LESLIE LEFT BRIGHTWATER A YEAR AGO. WE ARE PARTNERS NOW. COME SEE US SOON.
>
>   JOY

So, Leslie had left Brightwater and had turned the Buckskin Saloon—his half—over to Joy.

How could Buckskin Frank Leslie have resumed his travels from town to town without the news having been heard by either himself or Rick Hartman? Why had Leslie left Brightwater? That question Clint could answer himself. He was surprised that the man had stayed in one place for more than three years. He certainly could not have done the same himself.

Had Leslie been traveling under another name? Protecting himself from his reputation? Surely someone along the way would have recognized him. His long hair and mustache, his buckskin clothes—the man was too distinctive to have gone unnoticed for one year, let alone three.

Clint stood up and walked to Rick's table.

"These might interest you," he said, handing the telegrams to Rick.

"Where are you going?"

"I'm gonna turn in."

"And tomorrow?"

"I'll get an early start."

"To where?"

"Tylerville, to start. From there either New Mexico, or maybe Arizona."

"Brightwater?"

Clint nodded.

"Be careful, Clint," Rick said.

"I always am."

"There's a possibility you may not have considered."

"What's that?"

"Your friendship with Leslie is not unknown."

"So?"

"Somebody may be using this to set a trap."

"Who?"

"You've made a lot of enemies," Rick said, "and there are people you've never met who would like a chance to kill you."

"I know."

"And then there are your friends."

Clint frowned. "What's that mean?"

"I'm just telling you to be careful."

"Of my friends?"

"Of everyone."

Clint hesitated a moment, then turned to leave.

"Keep in touch," Rick said. "Let me know what happens and where you are. I'd like to keep an eye on you—sort of."

"Yes, Papa," Clint said. "I'll write every day."

As Clint walked away, Rick said under his breath, "You do that."

FIVE

Ron Diamond, known to some as the Diamond Gun, was in Denver, Colorado, when he heard of the death of Buckskin Frank Leslie. He'd been set to leave town the next day to head back to Duneden, Wyoming, where he had a little girl waiting for him.

He went immediately to the offices of the *Denver Post* and asked for the editor.

"What do you know about this story?" he asked the man, whose name was Fred Freidlander.

Freidlander looked at the big man with the salt-and-pepper hair and said, "As you can see, sir, it was picked up from another newspaper."

"The *Tylerville Gazette*," Diamond said. "I've never heard of it."

"An ex-reporter of mine is the editor," the man explained, "and I was just trying to help the paper out by picking up the story and running it. I've done so a few times in the past."

"But this story doesn't say anything," Diamond

pointed out. "It doesn't say how or where Buckskin Frank Leslie was killed."

"Perhaps not," Freidlander said, "but the man's name does have some value as far as selling papers is concerned, and that is what we are in business for."

"I thought you were in business to tell people the news," Diamond said. "You don't even know if the damned story is true, do you?"

"Uh, no."

"Then how could you print it?"

"As I told you," the man tried to explain, "I'm in business to sell—"

"Jesus!" Diamond said with contempt. He left the man's office before he gave in to the overwhelming urge to throttle him.

Ron Diamond had a friend named Clint Adams, and he knew that Clint was friends with Buckskin Frank Leslie. He also knew that Clint and Leslie were partners in a saloon in Brightwater, Arizona.

He was two weeks from home, but he was also two weeks from Brightwater. Clint Adams had helped him out during two rough periods in his life, particularly when his wife had been killed.* Maybe he'd been presented with a chance to pay the man back.

He left the offices of the newspaper and headed for the nearest telegraph office.

*THE GUNSMITH #52

SIX

In his room that night, Clint wished that he had taken one of the girls back with him. As it was, he was simply lying on his back on the bed, staring at the ceiling and wondering how many different kinds of fools he'd been for not keeping in closer contact with Frank Leslie. For God's sake, he *liked* the man, they were *partners*. Couldn't he have stopped into Brightwater in three years?

Leslie had left Arizona a year before. What frame of mind had he been in when he left, Clint wondered. The only way he was going to find that out was by going to Brightwater and talking to Joy Darling.

He turned on his side, intent on making an effort to sleep, when there was a knock on his door. One of the girls from the saloon? He hoped so.

He crossed the floor and opened the door. It was a woman, all right, but not someone he would have expected.

"Brianne," he said, in surprise.

"Hello," she said, smiling. She had combed her hair, applied some makeup—though not nearly as much as the girls at the saloon wore—and he could detect the scent of a subtle and not unpleasant perfume.

"Are you going to ask me in?"

"Brianne," he said, "I don't know if this is such a good idea. Gap is a friend of mine."

"Gap is a dear," she said. "He doesn't mind, believe me."

He did, so he stepped back to let her in.

She was wearing a simple dress that buttoned up to her neck and a shawl, which she discarded, letting it fall to the floor as she turned to face him after he had closed the door.

"I heard you're leaving town tomorrow."

"Yes, I am."

"Well, I didn't want to miss my chance," she said. "Who knows when you'll be back, and who knows where I will be when you return? Do you understand?"

"I understand," he said, "perfectly."

She moved against him then, bumping him with her firm breasts, and they kissed. He moved his hands down to the folds of her dress and lifted them up until he had his hands on the bare skin of her thighs. He moved his hands higher to cup her broad ass and found that she wore no underthings. She moaned and pressed herself against him as their tongues moved together. Her hands were on his shoulders, and she moved them down to his chest and pushed herself away from him breathlessly.

"Wait," she said. She backed up and began to

unbutton her dress. He watched as she undid them all and then slipped from the garment. Her bare breasts came immediately into view; she had wore nothing underneath on top, either. Her breasts were full and firm, her nipples dark and high on her breasts, making the undersides look especially full. He moved forward and cupped her breasts, testing their weight. He popped her nipples with his thumbs, and she moaned again.

"I'll wait on the bed," she whispered, and when she was reclining on it, she added, "I want to watch you undress."

He had pulled on his pants to answer the door, so all he had to do now was slip out of them. With the raging erection he had, taking them off was a little more difficult than pulling them on had been, but he did it and joined her on the bed.

She was on him then, eagerly moving about his body with her mouth. Finally, she settled on his rigid penis, covering it with kisses, popping the swollen head in and out of her mouth, and then suddenly engulfing him, taking most of him into her mouth and sucking him avidly. He lifted his hips off the bed and was surprised at how quickly she brought him to completion. It must have been the abruptness of her appearance and the feverish quality of the way in which she attacked him.

"Mmm," she said, moving up to lie next to him, "that was wonderful."

"For me, yes," he said.

"Oh, for me too," she said. "I enjoyed that almost as much as you did, but I *am* looking forward to some more active participation from you."

"In that case," he said, sliding his hand over
her sweat-slickened belly, "I won't keep you waiting."

He moved over her and began to lick and kiss
her breasts, enjoying the salty taste of her breasts.
He sucked her nipples, and when she extended her
arms up over her head, he quickly moved into her
armpits with his tongue, licking the sweat from
there too.

He felt her shudder, and she said, "Jesus, no
man has ever done *that* before," and he knew he'd
brought her to an orgasm already, albeit a small
one.

He moved back to her breasts, pushing them
together at one point so that he could suck on both
nipples at the same time. She moaned and cried out
his name when he did that, digging her heels into
the bed.

He moved further down, working his lips and
tongue over her belly and down to the dark tangle
of hair between her legs. The smell of her was
sharp, and he eagerly ran his tongue over her, tast-
ing her juices. She moaned and began to move her
butt as his tongue slid over her and *into* her. Finally,
he fastened his lips onto her clit and lashed it with
his tongue. She cried out and came violently, press-
ing her crotch tightly against his face.

He had a rock-hard erection again, and he
roughly turned her over. Before lifting her butt, he
ran his lips and mouth over her cheeks, finding them
firm and smooth. He lifted her onto her knees then,
and the broadness of her butt was an inviting target.
She wiggled it at him and he growled, then slid his

penis between her thighs and up into her wetness in one swift, violent motion. She almost screamed as he entered her, but then she braced herself against the bedposts as he drove into her from behind. He reached around to cup her breasts and tweak her nipples as he slammed into her. She began to babble, speaking so fast that he could not catch the words. Still, the sound of her mindless chatter seemed to urge him on, and he slid his hands from her breasts to her hips, holding her there and pulling her to him every time he drove into her. ·

They both came together this time, and then he withdrew from her and lay on top of her, kissing the back of her neck and running his hands over her buttocks and back. He turned her over and saw for the first time that her freckles extended down into the valley between her breasts. He began to lick them, and she laughed throatily and said, "They don't come off."

"Give me some time," he said.

"How much time?"

"How about all night?"

She closed her eyes and said dreamily, "You've got it."

He woke the next morning, surprised at how soundly he had slept. They had made love one other time during the night, and then they had both slept until morning.

He rolled over now and looked down at Brianne. In repose, her face was much plainer than when she was awake. It was her vitality that animated her features and made them more than plain. This was a woman who was beautiful on the inside, and any fool with two good eyes would be able to see that, despite her somewhat plain appearance.

"Why are you looking at me?" she asked.

"I'm admiring you."

"I must look a sight," she said, covering her face with both hands. The movement lifted her breasts, and he switched his gaze to them.

"You look wonderful."

"Oh, sure."

He leaned over and kissed her breasts, and she dropped her hands from her face to cup his head as he began to lick her nipples.

"You're a lovely woman, Brianne," he said. "Don't ever believe otherwise."

"You make me feel that way," she said. "For that I thank you."

She took hold of his face and lifted it so she could kiss him.

"Oh, look!" he said, glancing down at her breasts.

"What?" she asked, sounding alarmed.

"The freckles are gone."

She smiled and said, "You goon. Make love to me again before you leave. You make wonderful love, Clint Adams."

He buried his face in her breasts as he said, "I have a good partner."

SEVEN

Tylerville, Texas, had the look of one of those towns that was trying its best to grow but not doing a very good job of it. Clint was sure that the *Tylerville Gazette* was just the latest of the town's attempts to give itself some importance beyond just taking up space.

Clint rode down the main street at noon and found there wasn't much traffic. He was about to ask directions to the livery stable when he saw it. He rode up to it and called out for someone.

A man in his fifties, dragging a leg that was either dead or made of wood, came out and peered up at him, wiping his hands on a rag.

"Help ya?"

"I'd like to put my horse up."

"For how long?"

"Today, maybe overnight. I'm not sure about that yet."

"Have to charge you a day in advance."

"Do what you have to do," Clint said, dis-

mounting. He removed his rifle and left his saddlebags. If he were staying he'd come back for
them.

He paid the man for a day and said, "Leave those
saddlebags with the saddle. I want to be able to
find them if I need them."

"Sure."

"And don't go through them."

"What do you think I am?" the man asked,
indignantly.

"A stranger, and I say that to all strangers, so
don't take it personally. Is there another saloon
besides the one I passed?"

"We're building another one, but so far that's
the only one."

"Thanks."

Clint walked away from the livery toward the
saloon. On the way he passed several buildings that
were under construction. He assumed that one of
them—probably the largest—was meant to be the
new saloon.

As he reached the saloon he saw that the sheriff's
office was right across the street. He had not yet
seen the offices of the *Tylerville Gazette*.

He entered the saloon and walked to the bar,
which was against the front wall rather than one of
the side walls, which was unusual. The other thing
that was unusual for a town this size was the size
of the saloon. Physically, the saloon was much
larger than he might have expected. Unfortunately,
they had not yet put in enough furniture, and it
looked more like a saloon whose floor had been
cleared for a dance or a meeting of some sort.

"Howdy," the bartender said.

Clint looked at the bartender, who was wearing a boiled white shirt and a black string tie. He was a young man with a pronounced Adam's apple and a wide smile affixed to his pock-marked face.

"Beer," Clint said, "cold."

"Sure."

"Big place," Clint said as the bartender gave him his beer.

"The whole town is growing," the bartender said. "We'll be moving right up with it, too. Pretty soon we'll have some real gambling tables in here."

"Got some competition coming soon, I hear."

"Not really," the man said, his smiling getting wider. "We own that one, as well."

"You own this place?"

"Well, no," the young man said, sheepishly. "I mean Mr. Duggan—he owns this place and the new one."

"I see."

"You passing through or staying awhile?" the man asked.

"Just passing through," Clint said. "Who's your sheriff here?"

"We got us a new one," the man said. "Sheriff Dusty Rhodes."

Clint had heard of Rhodes. He was a career lawman who was probably approaching the age at which he'd be looking for a quiet job like this one.

"I read a copy of your local paper not long ago," Clint said. "Where would their offices be?"

"They got an office around the corner."

"Not on the main street?"

"No," the man said, "at least not until their new office is finished."

"That one of those buildings under construction I passed between here and the livery?"

"Yessir. They're gonna have them some real nice offices."

"That's nice," Clint said. "Will I find the editor over there now?"

"C.Z. White, yessir," the bartender said. "You looking for some work, by chance?"

"No," Clint said, "just some conversation." He paid for his beer and said, "Thanks. The beer was fine."

"Come back later, friend," the man said. "We got the prettiest gals in the county working here."

"Maybe I'll take a look," Clint said. "Where'd you say the *Gazette* office was?"

"Go out the door, make a right, and then make your first right. It ain't too impressive looking now, but it will be."

"I'm sure it will."

Clint left the saloon and headed for the newspaper office. If he could get the answers he wanted right away, he might not have to spend the night in this town. He wanted to get to Brightwater as soon as possible.

EIGHT

The young bartender had been right. The offices of the *Tylerville Gazette* were not at all impressive. In fact, Clint was surprised that the structure was even still standing. He stopped in front of the place for a moment, wondering if he should even risk his neck by entering the building.

Finally, he entered because his answers—or his lack of answers—were inside.

There was a boy of about fourteen working an ancient press, cursing at it, presumably to keep it running. He was tall and gangly, with a mass of red hair that fell across his forehead.

As Clint watched, the press suddenly stopped working. The boy shouted, "God *damn*!" and then looked around quickly to see if anyone had heard him.

"Oh!" the boy said when he saw Clint.

"I won't tell anyone, if you won't."

"It's just this da—this machine. Uh, can I help you with something?" the boy asked, nervously

rubbing his hands alongside the legs of the coveralls. Beneath the coveralls he did not wear a shirt,
and his hairless chest was somewhat pitiful.

"I'd like to see the editor, C.Z. White."

"Oh, sure," the boy said. He raised his head,
turned and shouted, "Mom!" When there was no
answer, he called again, "Hey, Mom?"

"Does your mom also work for the paper?" Clint
asked.

The boy frowned at Clint and said, "Well, sure,"
as if it were a silly question.

There was some movement from the back room,
and then Clint saw the woman come out. She was
also wearing coveralls, except that she had a shirt
underneath—unfortunately.

Although she was easily in her early forties, Clint
thought she was an extremely good-looking
woman, with a good body beneath the coveralls.
She had the same red hair as the boy, with a lock
falling down over her forehead.

"What are you shouting at?" she asked. "And
why isn't this press running?"

"The da—the darn thing stopped again."

"Well, get it started again."

"This feller wants to see—"

"I want to see the editor," Clint cut in. " C.Z.
White?"

"Yeah?" she said, frowning at him. "What
about?"

"Can I see him?"

"You're seeing him," the woman said. "I'm
Carole White."

"*Carole* White?"

"That's right," she said. "Is there something wrong with that?"

"No, no," Clint said, somewhat awkwardly, "not at all. Uh, what's the Z stand for?"

"I'd have to know you a whole lot better before I told you that, mister," she said. "A *whole* lot better. Now, what can I do for you?"

At that moment the boy managed to get the press started again, so Clint had to shout in order to be heard over the noise.

"Is there someplace we can go to talk?"

"What about?" she shouted.

Clint made a motion with his hands, indicating that he couldn't hear.

"Let's . . . outside . . ." he caught, then followed the woman out, where the noise was considerably less.

"Now, I've got a lot of work to do, mister, so what do you want?"

"Are you always this polite?" he asked.

"I don't have time to be polite," she said. "I'm trying to build a newspaper."

"It looks to me like you've got a long way to go."

"And just what does that mean?" she demanded, hands on hips.

He fished the newspaper article on Frank Leslie from his pocket and handed it to her.

She read it, then looked at him. "So?"

"That article doesn't say a whole heck of a lot."

"It says what I know."

"For a fact?" he asked. "You know for a fact that Frank Leslie is dead?"

She opened her mouth to answer, then stopped and studied him for a moment.

"Just what business is this of yours?"

"Frank Leslie is a friend of mine."

"Really?"

"Yes."

"And you know for a fact that he's alive?"

"No, I don't," Clint said. "I haven't seen him in three years."

"Oh, so you and he are *really* good friends, huh?"

"Look, lady—"

"Mister, I don't know who you are."

"My name is Clint Adams."

"All right, Mr. Clint Adams—wait a minute." Clint knew what was coming. "*Clint* Adams?"

"That's right."

"*The* Clint Adams?"

"I don't know what that means."

"Oh, don't be so modest, Mr. Adams," C.Z. White said. "You're the Gunsmith."

Clint didn't respond.

"Do you deny it?" she asked, as if she had trapped him in a lie or something.

"No, I don't deny it," Clint said, then remained silent after that.

"Sonofabitch!" she said, and Clint saw where her son had learned his language. She looked him up and down like a horse looking at a salt lick. She was a newspaperwoman who thought she was looking at a big story.

"What the hell are you doing in Tylerville?" she asked him.

"I came here to see you."

"Me? About what?"

"We're back to that again," he said. "I'm here about this article on Frank Leslie."

"Oh," she said, "that."

"Can I buy you a cup of coffee somewhere, Miss White?"

"*Mrs*. White," she said. "I'm a widow."

"I'm sorry," he said. "How about that cup of coffee? Maybe we can talk to each other a little more civilly."

"All right," she said. "Let me get cleaned up a bit first."

"I'll wait right here," he promised.

As she reentered the office, he heard the press stop again as the boy said, "God damn it!"

NINE

Carole White took Clint to a brand new cafe, where the floorboards were so new they still smelled like fresh pine trees.

"This town is really sprucing itself up, isn't it?" Clint asked.

"It's trying," she said. "Unfortunately, we have an idiot for a mayor, and unless we can get rid of him, I don't think this town is going to amount to much. Not while he's mayor."

"I understand you've hired Dusty Rhodes to be sheriff," Clint said.

"You know Rhodes?" she asked.

"I know of him," he said. "It's not a bad move for a town on the rise."

"All right," she said, "so the idiot made *one* good move."

"How did you come to be the editor of the *Tylerville Gazette*?" he asked.

"I worked as a reporter in Denver. My editor heard about this town, and he knew that I wanted to edit my own paper. Also, it was time for me to leave Denver. My husband had been killed and . . .''

"I'm sorry," Clint said quickly. "You don't have to talk about that."

"Actually, yes, I do," she said. "It's a painful thing, but the more I talk about it the angrier I get, and the angrier I get the more I believe that the bastard deserved what he got."

"I beg your pardon?"

"He was killed in bed," she said, making fists out of both hands, "with someone else's wife. The husband came home, found them, and shot them both."

He stared at her for a moment in shock, then said, "What a fool."

"You said it," she said. "He should have made sure the husband was out of town or something."

"I mean he was a fool to think he needed another woman."

She looked at him for a few moments, then said, "Uh, thank you," awkwardly.

"More coffee?"

"Thanks."

He poured her some from the pot, then poured himself another cup, even though it was probably the vilest coffee he'd ever tasted.

"Can we talk about why I'm here?" he asked.

"Sure."

"Frank Leslie and I were partners in a saloon in a town called Brightwater, Arizona," he said. "I didn't know that he'd even *left* Arizona, so you can imagine my shock at hearing that he was dead.

Consequently, I want to find out as much as I can about it.''

"Sure," she said, not meeting his eyes. "I don't blame you."

"Carole—can I call you 'Carole'?"

"Sure."

"Carole, I'd like to know where you heard the story."

"From a source."

"What source?"

"Clint—"

"Carole, this isn't Denver," he said, "and I'm not asking you to reveal some sort of a political source. I'm only asking you where you heard that Frank Leslie was dead. Is that too much to ask?"

Carole made a face and scratched her right eyebrow for a few moments.

"It's not too much to ask," she said. "It's just a little . . . embarrassing."

"Why?"

"Well, in my haste to get a jump on a story, I failed to accurately check out the source and thus the story."

"Who was the source?"

"A man who rode through town," she said.

"What man?"

"A bounty hunter."

"What was his name?"

"His name was Gary Carter."

"I never heard of him. What did he tell you?"

"Well, I heard from a local source that this feller Carter was telling people in the saloon that Buckskin Frank Leslie had been killed down south."

"Down south?"

"That was what I initially heard," she said. "Then I went after this Carter to find out as much as I could about Leslie's death."

"And?"

"Well," she said, "he seemed more interested in me than in talking about the story."

"Don't look so surprised," he said. "That's understandable."

"Well . . ."

"Go on," he said. "What did he say?"

She fidgeted uncomfortably in her seat. "He said he *heard* that Frank Leslie had been killed."

"How?"

"Shot."

"Where?"

"In New Mexico . . . somewhere."

"Somewhere?"

"I told you it was embarrassing."

"Why would you do such a thing?" Clint asked. "Especially when you're trying to establish your newspaper's credibility?"

"I needed *something*," she said. "I needed a scoop, and Frank Leslie, although he's kept a low profile over the past few years, was a name that would attract attention."

Clint stared down into his coffee cup.

"Look, Clint," Carole said, "I'm sorry I didn't substantiate the story, but I felt I had to go with what I had."

"You realize that this could just be a rumor?"

"Yes," she said, though she didn't comment any further.

"Tell me, did this bounty hunter, Carter, talk to the sheriff?"

"More vice versa," she said. "The sheriff had a talk with him."

"How long was Carter in town?"

"Just a couple of days."

"And where did he go from here?"

"I . . . don't know."

Clint was at a loss. He liked Carole White and he wished her well with her newspaper, but he was terribly disappointed in what she had to tell him.

"What will you do now?" she asked.

"One of two things," Clint said. "I've either got to go to Brightwater or just travel into New Mexico and start looking."

"For what?"

He looked up at her and said, "For Frank Leslie or his grave."

TEN

After coffee Clint and Carole White left the restaurant together. They stopped on the boardwalk outside.

"What's your next move?" she asked.

"I'll go and talk to the sheriff and see if he found out anything from this feller Carter."

"And then?"

"Well," he said, looking at the sky, "I'll guess I'll spend the night here and then push on in the morning."

"I feel . . . bad about this," she said. "Could I . . . buy you dinner tonight, before you leave?"

He looked down at her. She stood about five foot five, and her red hair was just starting to show some gray. She was wearing a man's shirt that was smudged with ink and a pair of jeans.

"On one condition," he said.

"What's that?"

"You wear a dress."

She smiled and said, "All right, I promise."

"I'll come for you at seven."

"Come to the shop," she said. "I'll be there until then."

"All right," he said, "see you later."

He watched her walk off down the street, a woman trying to make it in the world after being slapped in the face by a philandering husband who had the nerve not only to cheat on her but to get killed doing it. Maybe he could forgive the desperation that must have caused her to jump on the Frank Leslie story.

Maybe.

Clint walked back to the saloon and then crossed the street to the sheriff's office. Apparently the town had not yet felt the need to supply their new sheriff with a new office. This building was as old as the office of the *Gazette*. To be fair, maybe he was going to have an office in one of the buildings under construction.

During the walk Clint went over what he knew about Dusty Rhodes. He'd never heard any stories about the man that would approach legendary propositions, but he had always heard that he was a steady, trustworthy lawman who did his job. Those were probably the peacekeepers that the old West needed for years, not the Hickoks and Earps, the Bear River Tom Smiths and Clint Adamses, who overshadowed the law with their own reputations.

He opened the door and entered. The man behind the desk looked up with sharp blue eyes and narrowed them slightly as Clint closed the door and approached his desk.

Seated, Dusty Rhodes looked like a big man. Big, sloping shoulders, a thick neck, a head of gray-white hair worn short. He looked like a man in his late forties or early fifties, and he looked like a man who had gone face first into a lot of his jobs. There were scars on his forehead, and one of his eyebrows was almost gone.

"Can I help you?" the man asked.

"Sheriff Rhodes?"

"That's right." Rhodes was chewing tobacco, and he chose that moment to lean over and let loose a stream that hit a spitoon next to his desk with a resounding splash.

"My name is Clint Adams."

Rhodes stopped chewing for a moment, then heaved his bulk out of the chair and extended his hand. Standing, he looked fat, but Clint could see that the bulk was solid, not soft.

"Right nice to make your acquaintance, Mr. Adams," Rhodes said. "I've heard of you, naturally. What brings you to Tylerville?"

"I'm looking into a story I read in your local newspaper a while back."

"What story might that be? Have a seat."

Rhodes sat back down, and Clint seated himself in the hard-backed chair across the desk from him. He took the clipping from his pocket and handed it over. The sheriff read it and then, nodding, handed it back.

"I read that."

"I've already talked to Mrs. White about it. She told me that the story was carried here by a bounty hunter name of Carter."

"Gary Carter," Rhodes said. "I talked to the man when he was here."

"Did he say anything more about this?" Clint asked. "Anything that's not in the story?"

"We didn't talk about that, actually."

"What *did* you talk about? . . . If you don't mind my asking," Clint added.

"Him," Rhodes said. "I told him I didn't want him in my town. Have you ever heard of him?"

"Can't say as I have."

"He operates in Texas and New Mexico, mostly. He's got a bad reputation."

"Bad, in what way?"

"Most of his bounties come in slung across their saddles."

"*Most* hunters seem to have that particular reputation," Clint said. "What makes him worse than most?"

"I can't prove nothin', mind you," Rhodes admitted, "but he's been known to set up a lot of his quarry and then pick them off, like you might pick off some tin cans in target practice. I got no trouble with a man who *needs* to shoot to defend himself against scum, but I hold no truck with murderers, and in my book, that's what Gary Carter is."

"Would you say he was a liar as well?"

"Wouldn't put it past the man."

"Then he could have been lying about Frank Leslie being dead."

"Could have," agreed Rhodes, "but you couldn't prove that by me. We just didn't talk about that."

"I see," Clint said. "Well, I guess I'd better get myself a hotel room."

"Will you be staying long?" Rhodes asked. It was more than just a friendly inquiry, Clint knew. The man was working now.

"No, Sheriff," Clint said, standing. "I'll be moving on in the morning."

Rhodes nodded.

"Sorry I couldn't help you more, Mr. Adams," Rhodes said. "Was Leslie a friend of yours?"

"He was."

"Well, for your sake, I hope you find him alive."

"So do I, Sheriff," Clint said. "Thank you."

Clint left the sheriff's office and paused on the boardwalk outside. He decided to go to the livery to fetch his saddlebags and then go over and register himself at the hotel. If he was going to have dinner with Carole White that evening, he was going to need a bath.

ELEVEN

C.Z. White was nervous.

It was six months since the death of her husband, to whom she had been married for sixteen years. In all those sixteen years she had never even looked at another man. She was no blushing virgin when she'd gotten married at twenty-six, but it was a long time since she had been with a man other than her husband.

"Momma!" Zack, her son, said as she came out of her office wearing a dress.

"What's wrong with it?" she asked, looking down at her dress.

"Nothing," Zack said. "You look beautiful."

Carole embraced her son, kissing him on the forehead.

"Aw, Momma," he said, pulling away.

"Oh, I forgot," she said, tousling his already tousled hair. "You don't like that mushy stuff, right? Unless it was coming from Cindy Carrington, right?"

Cindy was a sixteen-year-old, cornfed beauty whom Carole knew Zack had his eye on. Cindy, precocious at best, teased most of the boys in town, and Carole was worried that Zack might be getting into something he was not prepared to handle. Still, he was at the age where a lot of boys lost their virginity in a hayloft, and he *had* grown up a lot over the past six months.

"Where are you going?" he asked her.

"To dinner."

"With who?"

"Clint Adams."

"Momma," he said, his tone one of awe, "is he really the Gunsmith?"

"Yes, Zack, he really is," she said.

"Are you gonna get a story?"

Smoothing down the front of her dress, Carole White said, "I hope so, Zack."

"Is that the only reason you're going to dinner with him?" her son asked, a crafty glint in his eye.

"Now what do you mean by that, young man?"

"You know what I mean," Zack said.

"You get this press running and don't leave here until you have every page run off, understand?"

"I understand, Momma," Zack said. Grinning, he added, "You have a good time."

Carole made a face at her son and went back into her office.

Actually, she did hope to get some kind of story from Clint that night, but that was not the only reason she was going to dinner with him. It had been a long time since she'd been with a man, and she certainly wasn't going to pick someone from this one-horse town. She had an itch, and had had it for some time, although one not bad enough to just pick anyone. Clint Adams, however, had increased that itch for her. He was just what she needed: an exciting man who might bed her one night and leave town the next.

That was all she was looking for.

That, and a story.

Clint Adams thought he knew what Carole White wanted from him.

Unless he was sadly—or *gladly*—mistaken, she was looking for a story from him. All newspeople, from another lady editor from his past, J.T. Archer,* on, seemed to see headlines whenever they met him, but he had no intentions of giving them to anyone. He'd never given them to J.T.— whose murder he had later solved in New York City**—and he wasn't going to give them to Carole White.

He hoped that she would understand, but the last thing he needed was a banner headline reading "The Gunsmith Searches for Killer of Buckskin Frank Leslie."

While he dressed after his bath, Clint wondered idly if Frank Leslie were alive somewhere, reading about his own demise with amusement.

Clint wondered what he would do if the newspapers ever announced his own death. It would be something to take advantage of. What harm would

*THE GUNSMITH #6
**THE GUNSMITH #48

it do for the world to think the Gunsmith was dead?
Sure, some of his friends would be upset, but he
could always contact them and let them know that
it was a mistake.

He laughed, thinking how Carole White would
feel about perpetrating a hoax like that on the reading public with his consent.

It would certainly be a story for her, wouldn't
it?

Sheriff Dusty Rhodes sat in his office for hours
after meeting the Gunsmith, Clint Adams. He'd
never met any of the great ones before, and to him
meeting Adams was the next best thing to meeting
Wild Bill.

As a young lawman he had been impressed with
legends. As he got older he felt that he was destined
to join them, but as the years passed it became
increasingly obvious that he would never be anything but a competent, steady lawman. He did not
have the flair of a Wild Bill or the mystique of a
Gunsmith.

Now, at fifty-one, he had to be content with being
the sheriff of Tylerville, Texas.

Just once, he wished—as he had done so many
times before—that he could be given a shot at the
job in Dodge City, Tombstone, or someplace like
that.

One last chance was all he needed to put his name
on the map.

He was no longer impressed with legends, because he knew them for what they were: men, like him, who had had better luck.

That was all it took, really, to become a legend.

Luck.

A lot of it.

TWELVE

Clint arrived at the *Gazette* office at just before seven and saw Carole's son talking to the printing press.

"More trouble?" he asked.

The boy whirled around, surprised, and then swallowed hard when he saw who it was.

"We weren't introduced," Clint said, putting his hand out to the boy. "I'm Clint Adams."

"I—I know," the boy stammered. He wiped his hand on his pants leg a few dozen times before taking Clint's hand. "I'm Zack White."

"Nice to meet you, Zack."

"Likewise . . . sir."

"Is your mother around?"

"She'll be out presently," Zack said.

"It looks like you and this press have an ongoing battle, eh?"

"Oh, yessir. The damn—uh, the *darn* thing seems to have a mind of its own."

"I guess you're just about the only one who can get it to run, huh?"

The boy looked embarrassed at first, then puffed out his thin chest and said, "I guess so. I'd better get to it if I'm going to get this edition out by morning."

At that point Carole White came out of her office. Clint was more than pleased by the sight of her. Twenty years before—or even ten—she must have been a breathtaking beauty. That kind of beauty had matured into a handsomeness that would stand her well into her fifties, where most raving beauties began to fade in their late thirties.

"You're early," she said.

"Five minutes," he said.

"Zack, I'll see you at home tonight."

"Sure, Mom." He called her "Momma" when they were alone and "Mom" when they were around other people.

"Shall we go?" she asked Clint.

"I hope you know a good place to eat."

"I know a surprisingly good place to eat," she said.

"Good," he said, "because I'm hungry."

Carole led the way, feeling that if she fed him well enough, he just might get into the mood to talk.

Carole took Clint to a restaurant she knew that served fine steaks, with all the garnish. To Clint's relief, the coffee was better than it was at the place they had gone to earlier in the day for their talk.

"I know what you want, you know," he said,

as they were having their after-dinner coffee. He'd decided to be frank with her.

"What's that?"

"A story."

"Doesn't every reporter and editor want that?" she asked. "Is that something I should be ashamed of? Fate drops the legendary Gunsmith into my lap and I'm not supposed to try and get a story?"

"Newspaperpeople," he said.

"What does that mean?"

"You're all alike," he said. "A one-track mind."

She sat back in her seat and stared at him. If he only knew what she really had on her mind. So far he had not made the slightest remark that might lead them to bed.

Maybe, she thought, she should be as frank with him as he was being with her.

"Clint?"

"Yes?"

"What will you do if you find that Frank Leslie *is* dead?"

"Is this an interview?" he asked.

"No," she said, "this is off the record."

"If he'd been killed," he said, "I'd try and find out who killed him."

"And when you did that?"

"I bring them to justice."

"Justice as prescribed by the law or as prescribed by the Gunsmith?"

He put his coffee cup down with a bang and she started, her eyes widening.

"What do you know about me?"

"O—only what I've heard," she admitted.

"Right," Clint said. "And does everything you've heard lead you to believe that I have my own special brand of justice?"

"Well, no," she said, "I just thought—"

"You thought what thousands of people think," he said. "That a man with a rep deserves it."

"You mean . . . you don't?"

"I'm not a mindless gunman, Carole," he said. "I don't kill for fun, and I don't kill unless I have to. I've never killed a man without a good reason."

"Is there a 'good' reason to kill a man?"

"The best reason in the world to kill a man is when he's trying to kill you."

"And every man you've ever killed was trying to kill you?"

"Or someone I cared about," he said. She opened her mouth to ask another question but he cut her off. "This is *really* starting to sound like an interview, isn't it? I'll bet when you were a reporter in Denver you were very good at your job."

"Believe me, Clint," she said, "none of this will show up in tomorrow's paper."

"Are you as good an editor as you were a reporter?" he asked.

"I hope to be."

He smiled. "You won't be," he warned her, "by making promises like that."

"I swear, Clint," she said again, "I won't use any of it."

Sure, Clint thought, tomorrow, but what about the day after that, after he was gone? What were the odds on his ever seeing a newspaper from Tylerville, Texas? They were even higher now, considering he'd already seen a copy once by accident. She could write whatever she wanted, sell her papers in Tylerville, and he'd never know it.

"Let's finish our coffee," he said, suddenly annoyed—with her and with himself. He wished he had moved on instead of deciding to spend the night. Maybe then he'd have been left with memories of Carole White as a woman who was just trying to survive. Now he was starting to think of her as he did most newspaperpeople: buzzards who picked a person clean just for a story and then went on to the next likely carcass.

THIRTEEN

Clint walked Carole back to her home, which was a couple of rooms she shared with Zack above the general store. The entrance was on the side and up a flight of steps precariously affixed to the side of the building.

"Is this safe?" he asked. It was the first words they had spoken since leaving the restaurant.

"Do you care?" she asked.

"What does that mean?"

"You think I'm just some avaricious newspaperwoman out to get a story from you."

"And what were you after tonight?"

She stared up at him and then said, "All right, I was after a story, but I certainly wouldn't trick you out of it. I'm not going to print anything you told me tonight. I wish you'd believe me."

"All right," he said. "I believe you."

"Do you, really?"

"Yes."

"Good," she said, seeming relieved. She looked

up the stairs and then back at him. "There . . . was something else I was after tonight."

"What's that?"

She moved closer to him, so that he could feel her body against his. When she kissed him, she was pressed so tightly against him that he could feel her nipples through the fabric of her dress.

"O God," she said, after the kiss, "I am so shameless."

"Carole . . ." he said, reaching for her.

"No, Clint," she said, putting her hands against his chest and pushing away. "I thought I was ready for this. I . . . I guess I'm not."

"I'll be leaving early in the morning," he said.

"I know," she said, her hands turning into fists. "Damn it, I know."

"Carole—"

"Good night, Clint," she said and hurriedly ran up the stairs.

He waited a few moments to see if she would come back out, and when she didn't he turned and walked toward his hotel.

Unfamiliar with the town, he decided to detour to the livery just to check on Duke. He found the front doors of the stable locked, but when he went around to the side he found that door open. If it had been locked he'd have gone to bed, secure in the fact that Duke was safely inside. He opened the door as soundlessly as he could and eased into the livery. If there were a thief inside, he didn't want to spook him.

Once inside, he could see a light and he heard

sounds—like someone . . . grunting, or moaning . . .

He moved further into the livery and quickly identified the sounds even before he saw them.

On a bed of hay, wrapped up in each other, were young Zack White and a somewhat plump blonde. Both were naked, and Zack was on top of the girl, his skinny buttocks rising and falling with increasing speed. The girl was moaning and talking to him, while Zack was grunting and groaning to the beat. Clint was sure from the sounds they were making that, although this was Zack's first time, it certainly wasn't the girl's. From what he could see of her, she was at least a couple of years older than the boy. Her plump thighs were spread as wide as they could get, and her hands were on his buttocks, trying to slow him down. She was probably the town cherry-buster, and young Zack was getting his well and truly busted this night.

Clint decided to leave them to it, and he withdrew from the stable to return to his hotel.

He was reclining on the bed twenty minutes later when there was a knock on the door. Maybe it was the blonde from the stable. Maybe she was going room to room now.

He opened the door and saw Carole White standing there somewhat sheepishly.

"I changed my mind," she said.

"Just like a woman."

She entered the room and said, "That's what I am tonight: a woman . . . not a reporter."

He smiled, reached past her, and closed the door.

• • •

Later they were lying side by side on the bed. It was obvious to him that she had not been with a man in a long time. There was a desperation to her lovemaking, as if it were not only a long time *since* she'd been with a man but that it would also be a long time until she was with a man again.

"God," she said.

He said nothing.

"When I got home Zack wasn't there."

"I know."

She turned her head and asked, "How do you know?"

"I saw him."

"Where?"

"In the livery stable."

"What was he doing there?"

He looked at her and said, "He was with a somewhat buxom young blonde on a bed of hay."

"O God," she said, covering her face with her hands. "Cindy Carrington. That little vixen, she's had her eye on him for some time."

"Well," he said with amusement, "she had more than her eye on him tonight."

"O God," she said, again, "my baby . . ."

"He's not a baby anymore, Carole."

"Well, he's certainly not a man, yet."

"He's more of a man tonight than he was earlier today."

"Is that what makes a man?" she asked.

"No," Clint said, putting his hand on her belly, "but it's a start."

Her belly was soft and not flat, with a small

roundness that she had to put up with because of her age. Ten years before it had probably been flat and hard, but now it was soft, though he didn't mind at all. Her hips and breasts were full, and he was willing to bet they had always been so.

She closed her eyes as he rubbed her belly, and he could feel her pulse quickening again.

"Why did you choose me?" he asked. "I mean, after all this time?"

"The truth?"

"Yes."

"Because you're leaving tomorrow," she said.

He slid his hand further down until the tips of his fingers were moist. She bit her lips and lifted her buttocks off the bed.

"That's probably the first totally honest thing you've said to me since I got here."

"Hey," she said, starting to protest, but he stopped her by sliding one finger fully into her. She gasped, and he captured her open mouth with his. . . .

Carole White slipped from the bed during the night and got dressed as quietly as she could.

"Leaving?" he asked, when she was fully dressed.

"You're awake," she said, accusingly.

"Have been for a while."

"And you let me sneak around here trying not to wake you?"

He smiled at her. "I enjoyed watching you dress."

She moved to the bed and sat down next to him.

She leaned over, put a hand on his bare chest, and kissed him, deeply and wetly.

"Come this way again," she said.

"In two or three years?"

"Well," she said, smiling, "don't make it quite that long."

"What are you going to do about Zack?"

She thought about it for a moment, then she shrugged and said, "I guess I'll have to let him grow up."

"Good choice."

"About that other thing . . ." she said.

"Hey," he said, taking her hand, "realistically speaking, what are the chances that I'll ever see another issue of the *Tylerville Gazette*?"

"Well, if things go as I plan," she said, "it will be sooner than you think."

"I wish you luck, Carole."

She kissed him again and then left quickly.

He rolled over and went back to sleep, breathing in the scent she left behind.

He was going to have to leave within the next two hours. His next stop was Brightwater, Arizona.

FOURTEEN

Joy Darling studied the account books that were sitting on her desk. Why, she wondered, was the Buckskin Saloon not making as much money as it had when Frank Leslie was running it?

She picked up her drink from the desk and sipped it. If she were going to be immodest, the reason could be that she no longer worked out front. Now that she was a full partner, she felt justified in simply running the place and no longer working in it. She had hired a girl to replace her, but maybe that girl was not as good at what she did as Joy had been.

Jesus, she thought, I hope this doesn't mean I have no head for business.

No, that wasn't true. Although they were not making as much money as they had when Leslie was there, they were still making a tidy profit. The Buckskin was the most successful saloon of the three in Brightwater, and it had been almost from the time Clint Adams had left Brightwater.

Clint Adams.

She sat back with her drink in her hand and thought about Clint Adams. She hadn't thought of him in a long time. After Clint had left, she and Leslie had drifted into a relationship that had been comfortable for both of them. She didn't think that love had ever entered into it.

Since Leslie had left she'd been with a few men, always from choice, but never with the satisfaction she had gotten from Leslie and from Clint before him.

She put her drink down and stood up. She had another desk down in her office, but she preferred to work up here, in her room. She walked to the full-length mirror against the wall, opened her robe, and dropped it to the floor. Beneath it she was naked. She studied herself critically. She was heavier than she had been when Clint was around, but her breasts had always been heavy and round, her very best feature. She cupped them now, hefting them. They were still nice and firm, and why not? She wasn't yet thirty years old. She turned and studied her buttocks. There was a time when they'd been flat, almost like a boy's, but more recently they had become full and round, like a woman's ass ought to be. Her body had filled out since she had abandoned the idea that she should never weigh more than one hundred and ten pounds. She now weighed a full, womanly one hundred and thirty, and she was even considering putting on another five pounds.

She checked the clock on her dresser and saw that it was almost four-thirty in the afternoon. Time for her to get dressed and go downstairs to see how business was doing.

Of course, by the time she was dressed to her satisfaction, it would be almost *five*-thirty.

FIFTEEN

Brightwater had changed very little, as far as Clint could see. Even at the time he had left, the town had fallen into a comfortable condition, and he guessed that the town fathers saw no reason for it to change.

As if he'd never left, he rode directly to the livery. The man who took Duke from him was a stranger to him, and he guessed that if the town *had* changed at all, it would be in the faces of the people who lived there. Not that he'd ever been all that friendly with a lot of them. He'd kept to himself for the most part, staying in the saloon with Frank Leslie and Joy Darling. Of course, there were Marlene Jory and Jesse Wells, and he wondered if they still lived in Brightwater.

He took his gear and walked to the hotel, where he registered and dropped his belongings in his room. He left the hotel and walked to the sheriff's office, hoping that Tom Sideman was still the law in Brightwater. He had never become friends with the man, but Sideman had been fair and competent.

He entered without knocking and saw Sideman standing at his coffee pot.

Sideman looked up and started to say, "I'll be right with you—" but when he recognized Clint he stopped short and stared.

"Hello, Sheriff."

"Clint Adams!" Sideman said. "Well, I'll be damned."

Clint was surprised by the reception he received. Sideman put down the pot and cup he'd been holding and crossed the floor, his right hand held out.

"It's good to see you," Sideman said, pumping Clint's hand. "What's it been, three years?"

"More like four."

"Four years, by God!"

Sideman had changed some. He was, if anything, even thinner than before. His hair had also thinned some, now that he was into his early forties. Clint also noticed that the man was wearing wire-rimmed spectacles. Behind them the brown eyes were still gentle, not the eyes of a lawman at all.

"Sit down, have a cup of coffee." Sideman got Clint a cup and handed it to him. "When did you get into town?"

"A couple of minutes ago."

"What brings you here?" Sideman asked, seating himself behind his desk.

"Frank Leslie."

"Frank?" Sideman said, frowning. "Frank left town a year ago, maybe more."

"I know that," Clint said. "I'm looking into a rumor that he's dead."

"Dead?" Sideman asked, sitting forward. "How? Where?"

"I've heard that he was shot down New Mexico way. I figured if anyone would know for sure it would be someone from here."

"Joy?"

"Possibly."

"You know she and Frank became . . . close after you left?"

"I would have expected that."

"Not that they were in love or anything," Sideman said, "but they were close."

"I'll go and see Joy after I leave here. Tell me, who else is still in town?"

"You must be thinking of Marlene Jory."

"Among others."

"Marlene left town soon after you did. Couldn't stand the shame, I guess."

Marlene's father, Sherman, was the banker when Clint had been there last, and he'd been as crooked a banker as you'd ever find. Clint had proved that, and Marlene had had to leave town after the scandal.

"And Jesse Wells?" Jesse had worked in the bank.

"Jesse is still here," Sideman said. "She still works in the bank. She and I have, uh, become . . ."

"Close?"

Sideman nodded, seemingly embarrassed.

"Well, that's fine," Clint said. "Jesse's a fine girl."

"Yes, she is," Sideman said. He looked at Clint and asked, "Clint, you're not—I mean, how long do you intend to be in town?"

"I haven't come back to renew *all* my old acquaintances, if that's what's worrying you," Clint said. "I just want to get as much information about Frank as I can, and then I'll be on my way."

"What kind of information?"

"Well, what frame of mind was he in when he left?"

"Not good."

"What do you mean?"

"Before he left, Frank had become bitter."

"About what?"

Sideman fidgeted in his chair.

"Come on, Tom," Clint urged.

"Well, to tell you the truth, Clint, I think he became jealous of you."

"Of me? Why?"

"Because he was here and you were out there. We read a lot about you, you know. I think he finally came to resent the fact that he'd been left here to . . . to tend bar or something."

"But that's silly," Clint said. "He came here to get away from being Buckskin Frank Leslie."

"I guess he found out that he preferred being Buckskin Frank Leslie. That's what he left here to do: become that man again."

"But if that was the case, how come I never heard of his leaving?"

Sideman shrugged and said, "Maybe nobody remembered him."

Clint rubbed his jaw. If Frank had left to resume

his old life and no one remembered, what would that have done to him? If Sideman were right and he was already bitter, what would he have become after that?

Clint finished his coffee and set it down on the desk, standing up at the same time.

"Are you going over to the Buckskin?" Sideman asked.

"Yes."

Sideman stood up. "Joy will be glad to see you," he said.

"It'll be nice seeing her, too. Tell me, do you still have the same mayor?"

"Ellis, yes," Sideman said, "and his daughter, Lucie, has become even more beautiful than she was when you left."

"She was . . . what, eighteen then?"

"Yes," Sideman said. "She's become quite a young woman, courted by every eligible man in town."

"You?"

"No," Sideman said, laughing, "not me. I'm happy with Jesse."

"Sheriff, it was good to see you," Clint said. The two men shook hands again.

"Stop in again before you leave."

"I'll do that."

Clint started for the door, and Sideman said, "Oh, by the way . . ."

"Yes?"

"There's another man in town who was interested in Frank Leslie."

"Is that right? Who?"

"Another rep," Sideman said. "His name is Ron Diamond. They call him the Diamond Gun. You know him?"

"Ron Diamond," Clint said, surprised. "Yes, I know him quite well."

"Friends?" Sideman asked.

"Yes, Sheriff," Clint said, "we're friends. You don't have to worry about Ron and me butting heads."

"Well, that's a relief," Sideman said.

"I'll be seeing you."

Clint left the sheriff's office, wondering what had brought Ron Diamond to Brightwater. Coincidence? Not likely. Clint did not believe in coincidence.

He stepped down from the boardwalk and walked toward the Buckskin Saloon.

SIXTEEN

It was early, and business was brisk. Joy Darling was beginning to think that maybe she'd simply made a mistake in the bookkeeping. Maybe she should hire a bookkeeper, but even when Frank had been there it was she who was keeping the books, and she knew she was good at it.

She walked to the bar and smiled at the bartender, Steve Owen.

"Business looks good today, Joy."

"Let's hope it gets even better tonight, Steve," she said. "Let me have a whiskey."

Owen would have made a comment about how early it was, but he could already smell the whiskey on her breath and knew that she'd already started up in her room. Besides, he'd already been warned about counting her drinks.

"Sure," he said, as he poured her a shot.

"Hey, little lady," a man's voice said as she prepared to drink it, "how about letting me buy you that little drink?"

Joy looked up at the man, a large, beefy customer with a thick neck and bad breath.

"Thanks, but it's already paid for."

"What'sa matter?" he asked, taking hold of her arm. "Ain't I good enough to buy you a drink?"

"Hey, friend," Owen said, "the lady is the owner. She doesn't work—"

"It's all right, Steve," Joy said, cutting him off. "Look, mister, there are plenty of girls on the floor for you to buy drinks for."

"I want to buy *you* a drink."

"Friend . . ." Owen began, but suddenly a gun appeared in the hand of a second man, who pointed it at the bartender.

"Shut up, bartender," the second man said. "My friend is talking to the lady."

Joy's eyes warned Owen not to start anything. She hoped that somebody would have sense enough to see what was going on and get Sheriff Sideman. Meanwhile, she had to keep these two talking. As long as they were talking, they wouldn't be shooting.

"Now, how about that drink, little lady?" the first man asked.

"Sure, cowboy," Joy said, "buy me a drink."

"Bartender," the man said, "pour the lady a drink."

"She's got a drink," Steve Owen said.

The man looked at the shot glass in Joy's hand and clumsily knocked it from her hand.

"She dropped her drink," he said. "Pour her another."

"Sure," Owen said, putting another shot glass on the bar.

"No," the man said, "pour her a *real* drink."

"What?"

"A bigger glass," the second man said. "Mr. Talman wants the lady to have a bigger glass."

Owen looked at Joy, who nodded.

"A beer mug," Talman said, "pour it into a beer mug."

Owen put a beer mug on the bar and then poured some whiskey into it.

"Fill it up," Talman said.

"W-what?"

The second man pressed the barrel of his gun against Owen's temple and said, "Fill it!"

The bartender upended the bottle of whiskey and filled the beer mug to the brim.

"There's your drink, little lady," Talman said. "Drink it."

"Why don't you have one with me?" she asked.

"I don't drink," Talman said. "That's why I like to see other people drink."

"It's not polite to make a lady drink alone."

"You sayin' I ain't polite?" he asked. He still had a hold of her arm, and now he squeezed until she winced from the pain. "I'm buyin' you a drink, ain't I? Don't that make me polite?"

"Sure, friend," she said, "sure. How about letting go of my arm. You're tearin' it off."

"I'm gonna tear it off if you don't drink!" he growled at her.

"You better do what the man says, miss," the other man said. "Drink."

Talman had her by the left arm, so Joy picked up the drink with her right hand, raised it to her lips, and sipped it.

"All of it," Talman said. "Drink it all down . . . now!"

Joy stared at him, her eyes wide, and then raised the mug and began to drink. She got halfway through it before she started to gag, and then she threw up on Talman's boots. The man leaped back with a cry.

"What the hell—you bitch!"

He raised his right hand to slap her and she cringed against the bar, but someone's hand locked around his wrist and pulled him back. Talman staggered, off balance, and fell to the floor.

"Wha—" the second man said, bringing his gun around.

"Stop right there," Clint Adams said.

"Shoot the bastard!" Talman said from the floor.

Clint executed a half-turn and kicked Talman in the jaw with the heel of his boot. Talman fell backward, his head hitting the floor hard, and he didn't move.

Clint turned his attention back to the man with the gun.

"Your friend's out of it, now," Clint said, "but you still have time to die."

"You're crazy," the man said. "I have my gun out."

"Then go ahead," Clint said, "make a move. It'll be your last, that I promise you."

The man with the gun stared at Clint as if he were crazy. This man's gun was still in his holster, and yet there was such a look of confidence in his eyes . . .

"Either make a move or holster it," Clint said.

The man studied him a few seconds longer, then slowly holstered his gun.

"Now pick up your friend and get out of here."

The man looked down at Talman, who was bleeding profusely from the mouth.

"He needs a doctor."

"Get him one," Clint said, "in the next town."

The man leaned over, took Talman under his arms, and slowly dragged him from the saloon. When they were gone, Clint turned to the bar.

"Clint Adams!" Steve Owen said, grinning.

"Hello, Steve."

"Clint who?" Joy asked. She was still slumped against the bar, and now she turned her head to look at Clint, except that her eyes wouldn't focus.

"Come on, Joy," Clint said, "let's go upstairs."

"Upstairs," she said. She released her hold on the bar and started to fall, but Clint caught her and lifted her easily into his arms.

"When she realizes it's you," Steve Owen said, "she's going to be real tickled."

"That won't be for some time, Steve," Clint said. "Can you run the show without her for a while?"

"Sure," the bartender said. "Take her on up and take care of her. She's in Frank's old room."

"Take care of me," she mumbled into his chest.

"I'll do just that," Clint said, and he carried her up.

• • •

The man seated at a table all the way in the back
of the saloon relaxed as the two toughs left the
saloon and watched in amusement as Clint caught
the falling woman and carried her up the stairs.

The time had not been quite right to announce
his presence when Clint Adams first entered the
saloon, and it had gotten worse from there. Clint
obviously knew both the bartender and the blond
woman, who apparently owned the place.

Ron Diamond decided to let Clint Adams renew
his old acquaintances before announcing his own
presence.

SEVENTEEN

"Ohhh, I feel like shit," Joy Darling moaned, and then, covering her face, she added, "and I must look worse."

"You look fine," Clint said, "you look beautiful."

"You're such a liar," she said, looking up at him from the bed. "It's so good to see you."

"It's good to see you, Joy," he said.

"You came in at just the right time, rushing to my rescue, like always."

He gathered her into his arms and hugged her while she cried.

"Why are you crying?"

"Because I'm glad to see you," she said into his chest, "and because I feel and look like shit."

She pushed away from him and said, "Go downstairs and wait for me."

"Joy, you're finished for the night."

"Nonsense," she said, wiping the tears from her face with her palms. "I'm going to take a bath and

89

make myself beautiful and then come back downstairs. You wait for me, you hear? Don't leave.''

''Are you sure about this?''

''Positive. Go,'' she said, waving him away,
''and wait for me.''

''All right,'' he said, standing up. ''We have a
lot to talk about.''

''I know we do,'' she said. ''Go on, get out and
forget you saw me like this.''

He wanted to remind her that he had seen her
looking worse. There was a very light scar on her
cheek as proof of that, but he decided not to bring
that up.

He left her room and went back downstairs. On
the way down, he saw Ron Diamond sitting at a
back table. He detoured to the bar for two beers
and then went to join Diamond.

''Hello, Clint,'' Diamond said, standing up.

The two shook hands and then sat back down.

''What brings you to Brightwater, Ron?'' Clint
asked.

''I was in Denver and heard some news about
Frank Leslie.''

''What news?''

''That he was dead.''

''You too?'' Clint asked. ''What paper did you
see it in?''

''A Denver paper, but they said they had picked
it up from some small Texas newspaper.''

''The *Tylerville Gazette*,'' Clint said. ''I was
there and met the editor. She said she used to work
in Denver.''

''That's what the Denver editor said.''

"Well, why would that news bring you here? You didn't know Frank."

"But you do," Diamond said. "I figured you'd come here, so I thought I'd come and wait for you. Been here a few days."

"I stopped a day in Tylerville or I'd have been here sooner."

"What did you find out?"

"Nothing more than was in that article," Clint said.

"It wasn't much of an article."

"And it was based on hearsay."

"Well, if you can't find something out here I'd say your next move would be to go to New Mexico and find out for yourself."

"That's my plan."

"Want some company?"

Clint was about to answer, but he stopped himself. Instead he asked, "How's Lisa?"

"Fine," Diamond said. "Beautiful."

"She must be waiting for you."

"I sent her a telegram," Diamond said. "I owe you, Clint, more than I can ever repay, but maybe this will repay some of it."

"Well," Clint said, "I suppose I could use the company. New Mexico's a long ride, and it's a big place to look for one man."

"Who may not want to be found."

"What makes you say that?"

"A man like Frank Leslie couldn't stay out of the newspapers unless he wanted to," Diamond said. "This is the first I'd heard of him in years."

"Well, he was here for years, but he left a year ago."

"And that didn't get a mention until now?" Diamond asked. "Believe me, Clint, I know about staying out of the newspapers."

"I know you do."

"I wonder why he would leave here, though, and simply settle down someplace else."

"I guess we'll have to ask him if and when we find him," Clint said.

Diamond nodded and sipped his beer. "How's your friend?" he asked, referring to Joy Darling.

"She's fine," Clint said. "She'll be down shortly."

"She's got a good constitution if she's going to come back down here after drinking all that whiskey. I was about to step in when you came along."

"I could have used your help."

"You did fine," Diamond said, "but I had you backed up, don't worry about that."

"I wouldn't have been worried," Clint said, "if I knew you were there."

They spent the next half hour or so catching up with each other, as they hadn't seen one another in well over a year. To Clint, Diamond seemed to be a changed man, one no longer laboring under the weight of his wife's murder. He attributed that to a little girl in Dundeden, Colorado, who had given his life new purpose.

After forty-five minutes, Clint heard a door close upstairs, even over the noise in the crowded saloon. He looked up and saw Joy appear at the head of the stairs. Her appearance was enough to hush some of the noise that was going on as the men in the room took notice of her.

How could they have helped it?

She appeared to be steady and sober, as well as clean and refreshed. She was wearing an even lower-cut dress than before—in Clint's honor, he was certain—and her rounded breasts were creamy and smooth. Her blond hair was piled high atop her head, showing off her long, graceful neck. As she came down the steps, she did so with exaggerated care, knowing that all of the men in the saloon were looking at her, though caring only that Clint Adams was looking at her for the first time in years.

"Well," Diamond said, "she certainly *looks* okay, doesn't she?"

That was an understatement.

She looked wonderful.

EIGHTEEN

As Joy Darling walked toward his table, Clint Adams had a thought: There was only one way a person could recover that quickly from that amount of whiskey, and that was if they'd had a lot of practice at it.

As she got closer he saw that she was just a little off balance, and her eyes were not quite focused. Other than that, she had recovered remarkably well.

Clint and Diamond rose as she reached them.

"Joy, I'd like you to meet a friend of mine, Ron Diamond."

"It's a pleasure, Mr. Diamond."

"The pleasure is all mine, ma'am," Diamond said. "You have a very nice place here."

"Thank you. Are you boys all right with your drinks?"

"We're fine," Clint said. "Will you sit with us?"

"I've got to circulate," she said, "but you and I will talk later, won't we, Clint?"

"Yes, we will."

She touched his arm and then moved on.

"I think that gal has more on her mind than just talk," Diamond said as they sat down.

"She was given this place by Frank when he left town," Clint said. "Half of it, that is."

"And who owns the other half?"

"I do."

Diamond's face did not betray the surprise he felt. "Did he tell her where he was going?" he asked.

"I guess that's one of the things we'll talk about," Clint said.

Clint watched as Joy worked the room and talked to her girls. He didn't recognize any of them, but of course the girls he knew when he was in Brightwater would be long gone by now. The one thing the saloon business had in common, no matter where it was, was the turnover in saloon girls.

As the evening wore on, Clint and Diamond accepted an offer from two other men to start a poker game, but during the game Clint kept his eye on Joy. He knew she had to be feeling at least a little sick from her experience, and yet she did not betray it. In fact, at one point he even saw her taking a drink.

If he remembered correctly—and he was sure he did—she didn't drink much when he first knew her. He wondered if the rigors of running this place for the past year had driven her to it.

Because he wasn't paying much attention to the game, he lost steadily. The stakes were small, so he was only down about forty dollars after a couple of hours. Diamond, on the other hand, was the winner. He had Clint's forty, plus another hundred from the other two men.

"We've had it," one of the men said.

"You're too good for us," the other said to Diamond.

"Any time, boys," Diamond said. "All contributions gratefully accepted."

As the two men left, Diamond leaned forward and said to Clint, "Your mind sure wasn't on the game. You want your forty dollars back?"

Clint waved him away. "You won it fair and square."

"You worried about your friend?"

"Yes."

"She seems pretty much in control to me."

"Too much in control," Clint said. "Something's wrong."

"Well," Diamond said, "I guess that's something else you'll have to talk about."

"And real soon, too," Clint said.

It was about half an hour to closing, he figured, but that last half hour seemed to drag by. Finally, Steve Owen, the bartender, had to start shooing people out. He made no move toward Clint and Diamond, because he was well aware of the fact that Clint was half owner of the Buckskin.

After he had locked the door on the last customer, the girls all gathered at one table and had a drink together. Joy walked over to the table Clint shared with Diamond and sat down.

"Marla's got her eye on you," she told Diamond.

"Oh, really?" he asked. He looked at the table full of girls and asked, "Which one's Marla?"

"The big blonde," Joy said.

Marla was big, all right. She had huge, round breasts that overflowed from her dress, and she was about five years from being fat.

"She'd be real comfortable to curl up with to-night," Joy promised him.

"I don't think so," Diamond said, smiling. "Would you kindly tell her for me that perhaps we can make it another time?"

"Sure," Joy said.

Diamond stood up and said, "I'll leave you two alone. I'm sure you've got a lot of catching up to do."

"Good night, Ron," Clint said.

"Stayin' at the hotel?" Diamond asked. When Clint nodded, Diamond said, "How about the dining room at nine o'clock for breakfast?"

"I'll meet you then."

"A real pleasure to meet you, ma'am," Diamond said to Joy.

"Please, call me 'Joy'," she said. " 'Ma'am' makes me feel so old."

"Good night, Joy."

Owen let Diamond out, and the girls started to go up to their rooms. Clint noticed that Owen was trailing one of them: one of the benefits of being a bartender.

"Well," Clint said, "we do have a lot of catching up to do, don't we?"

"Yes, we do," Joy said, "and I suggest we do it right—up in my room."

"Joy," he said, putting his hand over one of hers, "are you feeling—"

"I'm feeling fine, Clint," she said, smiling. "But in about five minutes I know I'm going to be feeling a whole lot better."

NINETEEN

It took less than five minutes.

As soon as they entered her room, Joy turned and pinned Clint to the door. Her breasts were solid against his chest, like two cannonballs, and her mouth was eager as she searched for his. She tasted of whiskey, but he quickly forgot that when her hands became busy.

They were naked on the bed moments later, and she was astride him, his rigid cock buried deep inside of her. She leaned forward to let her breasts dangle in his face, and he played with them, using his hands, his lips, his teeth, and his tongue. At one point he separated them, then released them and watched them slap together, flicking at the nipples with the tip of his tongue.

"I know," she said, breathlessly, "I'm bigger than you remember. . . ."

"Some," he said.

"And heavier."

"Some," he said, reaching around to grasp her buttocks, "but I'm not complaining."

"Oh, honey," she said, closing her eyes as he took control of the tempo, "neither am I!"

Holding her by the buttocks, he slowed her down, so that she was riding him in longer strokes, taking him in and then easing him out, but it soon became apparent to him that she didn't want to go slow anymore, so he released her and let her move at her own pace.

She began to bounce on him wildly, coming down hard each time and gasping as he penetrated her deeply, and then suddenly he was exploding and she was moaning and bouncing and scratching his chest as she closed her eyes, threw back her head, and climaxed with him. . . .

". . . So after Frank left, I just threw myself into running this place."

"And started drinking?"

He didn't think she was going to answer, but she surprised him—pleasantly—by admitting her problem.

"That didn't come until later, almost six months later. I'd never realized what went into running this place. Frank did it so well, so smoothly. It took me time to catch on, and then several months ago I realized we weren't making as much money as we had been when Frank was running the place."

"And you started to worry?"

"I shouldn't have, really," she said. "I just did the books today, and we're still *making* money, just not as much. I know I've got a responsibility to

you to try and keep the business at the same level
that Frank had it, or higher. . . ."

He reached over and put his finger to her lips to
quiet her.

"The only responsibility I want you to worry
about is the one you have to yourself. If you have
to slow down a bit to catch your breath, to take the
pressure off, to stop drinking, then do it."

"The profits would go down even more."

"To hell with the profits! If they go down, take
it off my end."

"I couldn't do that."

"I'm telling you to," he said. "If you're not
healthy, then this place is really going to go down-
hill, and then where will we both be?"

"Well," she said grudgingly, "I suppose you
have a point."

"You bet I do," he said. "No partner of mine
is going to work herself into the ground. Got it?"

She smiled in the darkness. "Got it."

They lay together for a while in silence, and then
she asked, "So what brought you here? Not that I
didn't expect you after that telegram."

He hesitated a moment, then said, "You haven't
heard the rumor?"

"Rumor about what?"

"About Frank."

"No," she said. "What's the rumor about
Frank."

"There's a rumor going around that he's dead."

She was silent for a moment. "That's crazy!
Where did you hear that?"

"Actually, I read it in a newspaper."

"In the paper?" she said, suddenly sounding concerned. She had that same attitude about written news that a lot of people had: If it was in print, it must be true. That was one reason Clint's reputation had grown the way it had—that's how all reputations grew in the press.

"There wasn't much in the way of facts, only that he had been killed in New Mexico. I came here to find out if you knew anything about it."

"No, nothing," she said. "I—why would I?"

"I thought Frank might have kept in touch."

"Yeah," she said, "that's what I thought for a while. But as the months went by, I resigned myself to the fact that he had just disappeared from my life—like you did."

"Joy . . ."

"I'm not asking for any apologies," she said. "That was just the way I felt for a while. Do you really think he's dead, Clint?"

"I don't know," he said, "but I'm going to have to find out. What was his frame of mind when he left?"

"Not good."

"What do you mean?"

"Well . . ." she began, hesitating.

"Come on, Joy," he said, prodding her, "I need the truth."

"He had become very bitter, Clint," she said. "And I think he was jealous of you."

"Of me?"

"Of your reputation," she said. "It's grown over the years, while he was 'tending bar,' as he said. So he was going out to do something about it."

"I can't believe this," Clint said. "Not of Frank."

"I don't know," she said. "Maybe it was being cooped up all day in the saloon and into the night, rousting drunks and all. It wasn't the life for a man like Frank—or you. Frank should have stayed in the office, but he always insisted on working the bar himself."

"Did he say where he was heading when he left?"

"No," she said, "he just . . . left."

So there it was. Joy had almost nothing to tell Clint that would help him. Now it was off to New Mexico for sure, where he'd try to find out the truth.

"What are you going to do?" she asked.

"Go looking for him."

"Where?"

"Where else?" he said. "Where he was supposed to have died."

"New Mexico?"

"Yes."

"When will you leave?"

He hesitated before saying, "Tomorrow."

"That soon?"

"As it turns out," he said, "I've wasted my time in Tylerville, as well as here."

"Well," she said, "I hope all of your time here wasn't wasted."

He slid one hand over her hips until he found her ass and then slapped her.

"You know what I mean."

"Yes," she said, "I do."

"Are you going to be all right?"

"Sure," she said. "You've taken some of the pressure off. You've made me realize that I should be running this place my way, not trying to replace Frank."

"I'm glad," he said.

"Do you think you'll be back this way . . . some time?" she asked.

"More often than before," he said.

"That's not saying much."

"I'm going to have to start checking on my interests here more often."

"Good," she said. "I'll start short-changing you so you have to come back."

He laughed and hugged her. She slid one leg over his and slid on top of him. She kissed him deeply, then began to kiss his chest.

"Clint?" she said after a moment.

"Hmm?"

"Will you let me know?" she asked. "If it's true, I mean. Will you let me know?"

"Sure, Joy," he said, wrapping his arms around her. "I'll let you know as soon as I know."

TWENTY

At seven o'clock the next morning, Clint slipped from Joy's room and went over to the hotel.

"Can I get some breakfast this early?" he asked the desk clerk.

"The cook's in," the clerk said. "I don't see why not."

Clint gave the clerk a dollar and said, "Be a good feller and run in there and ask him to whip up two breakfast specials."

"Don't you want to know what the special is?" the clerk asked.

"Just as long as it's good, filling, and the coffee is drinkable."

"Yessir."

Clint went upstairs and pounded on Ron Diamond's door until the man answered.

"What the hell—" Diamond began, then stopped when he saw it was Clint. "It isn't nine o'clock yet."

"You going to New Mexico with me?"

"Well, of course I am."

"Then get packed and head down to the dining room. We're leaving right after breakfast."

"You could give a guy a little more notice," Diamond complained, scratching his belly.

It was only then that Clint realized he had interrupted something. He looked past Diamond and saw Marla, the big-breasted blonde from the saloon, in Diamond's bed. Her hair was tousled and she was yawning and stretching, which was doing wonderful things to her big, pink-tipped breasts.

"I thought you begged off last night," he said to Diamond.

"You wouldn't believe it, Clint," Diamond said softly, "but she came to my room and practically begged her way into my bed. I tell you, a feller my age can't take very much of this."

Clint thought Diamond looked pretty good for a man who had to be fifty or more—and Marla looked anything but dissatisfied.

"Look," Clint said, "I'm going to be down in the dining room in fifteen minutes, eating. After that, I'm heading for the livery. You can catch up with me anywhere along the way."

"What about supplies?"

"We'll get them in the next town."

"Honey," the woman called from the bed, "Marla needs a wake-me-up."

"A wake-me-up?" Clint asked.

Diamond looked sheepish and said, "It'll probably be the death of me."

"Do what you can for her," Clint said, "but make it fast."

"At my age?" Diamond said.

"Stop giving me this crap about your age, Ron," Clint said. "Marla looks happy as a kitten."

"That may be," Diamond said, "but I'll tell you, it took some doing."

"You can tell all me about it," Clint said, "on the way to New Mexico."

As Clint Adams walked off down the hall, Ron Diamond turned and faced Marla. He'd been quite surprised when she had shown up at his door that night. Before he could decline, Marla had already slipped past him and divested herself of her clothes. At that point, there was hardly a man alive who could have said no.

Marla's appetite for sex had turned out to be quite diverse. First she had slithered down between his legs and almost gobbled him up, and then she had turned herself around, presented him with her smooth, wide butt, and demanded that they do it "doggy style." After that Diamond had been ready to go to sleep, but not Marla. She had washed him and then taken him in her mouth again. He hadn't thought she could do it, but in moments she'd had him hard as a rock again, and she'd hopped on. She was a heavy girl, and every time she came down on him she had squealed. It was all he could have done to keep from being crushed, but not once had he muttered a word of complaint.

After that she had allowed him to sleep for a few hours, until he'd woken up with her between his legs again. This time she'd said she wanted to be on the bottom, and he had dutifully allowed her to slide under him, and then he'd entered her and rode her hard.

The next thing he knew, someone was pounding on his door and it was Clint Adams.

Now he was facing Marla, who had tossed off the sheets in anticipation of her "wake-me-up." The girl had thighs the likes of which he'd never seen, and her skin was soft and smooth. The pink slit between her legs was already moist, and it beckoned to him silently, but insistently.

He felt the rise between his legs and wondered if Clint would allow him to take this creature with them to New Mexico.

She made him feel his age—and yet at the same time like a young bull again.

TWENTY-ONE

Clint had ridden through New Mexico on his way to Brightwater, Arizona, fully aware that he may have been wasting time by not just staying there. He'd felt it was necessary, though, to check out Brightwater, and the fact that nothing of use had been discovered did not change his opinion of the trip.

During his first passage through New Mexico, he had picked up newspapers as he rode through towns small and large and had perused them, looking for some kind of word on Frank Leslie. All he'd done was build up his collection of newspapers, which he'd finally just dumped along the road somewhere.

Now that he was in New Mexico again, this time with Ron Diamond, he hadn't a clue where to start.

They rode into Los Palos during midafternoon and stopped in front of the saloon. They meant to have a drink and then move on. It was simply a breather for them and for the horses.

In the saloon they each bought a beer and took a complimentary hardboiled egg, then sat at a table in the nearly empty saloon.

"Albuquerque," Ron Diamond said as they sat down.

"What?"

"Albuquerque," Diamond repeated.

"What about it?"

"It's a big town," Diamond said. "One of the biggest in New Mexico—that and Santa Fe—and we're closer to Albuquerque."

"And what do we do when we get there?"

"Look, listen," Diamond said and, raising his mug, added, "and have a few more beers and eat something more substantial than hardboiled eggs."

Clint studied his friend across the table. "Are you saying this because you want a soft bed and a good steak?"

"Well, of course," Diamond said, "but also because we don't know where else to go, do we?"

"No, we don't."

"And we *will* be able to get a good meal there, won't we?"

"Sure."

"And soft beds?"

"Sure."

"So what have you got against Albuquerque?"

"Nothing."

"Then we're going?"

"Sure," Clint said, "we're going."

"You're agreeing to this so easily?"

"Why not?" Clint said. "When you're right, you're right. I don't know where the hell I'm going, so maybe we'll find out something in Albuquerque."

"Shall we go, then?"

"Finish your beer," Clint said, "and your egg, and give the horses a few more minutes to catch their breath." He stood up. "I'm going to find a copy of this town's newspaper."

"See," Diamond said, reaching for the uneaten half of Clint's egg, "that's another thing: Albuquerque will have a much larger newspaper."

"I've already agreed to Albuquerque," Clint said. "You can stop trying to sell it, all right?"

"Sure, okay."

"Do you have money invested in that town or something?" Clint asked. He laughed and left the saloon in search of a newspaper.

Diamond continued to drink his beer and finished Clint's egg. While he was licking the salt from his fingers, a man came over and stood behind Clint's vacated chair.

"I know you," the man said.

Diamond looked up at him, appraisingly. Young, in his midtwenties, and full of himself. He stood with one hip cocked, his hand hanging loosely by his gun. On his face was an arrogant sneer, the kind Diamond used to like to wipe off faces in his younger days.

This young man was lucky that Diamond had mellowed with his old age.

"Do you?" Diamond asked pleasantly.

"Sure I do," the man said. "You're that—

what's your name? That feller with the diamonds. I can't remember your name, but I know it's got something to do with diamonds, ain't it?"

"I don't have any diamonds for you, son," Diamond said. "Why don't you just go back to your own business and get out of mine."

"No, no," the man said, "you don't understand."

"What don't I understand?"

The man straightened his back now and looked down his nose at Diamond. He raised his voice in order to attract as much attention as he could.

"I'm better than you!" he said.

"Fine," Diamond said, and looked back down at his beer.

"Hey, did you hear me?" the man said, louder now. "I said, I'm ... better ... than ... you!"

Diamond did not react.

"With a gun, I mean!"

No reaction.

"Hey, old man!" the boy said. "Don't you hear me?"

Without looking up, Diamond said, "I hear you, son."

"I said—"

"I said I heard you."

The man looked around, grinning at his two friends who were standing at the bar, posing for the few others in the saloon.

"So, uh, what do you intend to do about it?"

Diamond looked up at him now and said, "Nothing."

The man looked puzzled. "Whataya mean, nothin'?"

"Just what I said," Diamond said. "Nothing."

"Uh, ya can't just do nothin'," the man argued, frowning. "I mean, I said I was faster than you. Ain't you gonna prove I'm wrong?"

"No."

"Hey, come on," the younger man said, whining now. "You gotta try and prove I'm wrong."

"Why?"

"Why?" the young man repeated, beside himself now. "If you don't, everybody here will think you're yeller."

"So what?"

"Whataya mean, so what?" the man cried. "Don'tcha care if they think you're yeller?"

"I don't care what they think," Diamond said. "And I don't care what you think. If you want to think you're faster than me, go ahead. If they want to think I'm a coward, they can go ahead. *You're* the only one who seems to care what people think."

"What's going on?"

The young man turned at the sound of the voice and saw Clint Adams standing there, holding a newspaper.

"Are you his friend?" he asked.

"I am."

"Well, if he don't stand up and face me, he's yeller."

Clint leaned over so he could see Diamond around the other man. "You mind being yellow, Ron?"

"I don't mind a bit," Diamond said.

Clint looked at the young man and said, "He doesn't mind, I sure don't." He looked back at Diamond and said, "Time to go."

"I'm ready," Diamond said and stood up. As he walked past the young man, he patted him on the arm and said, "Sorry I couldn't accommodate you, son."

Diamond continued to walk away, and Clint saw that the young man, very agitated, was about ready to draw his gun.

"You draw that gun you're going to be dead in a second, son," he said. "I'm not as patient as my friend here."

Diamond turned and looked at the agitated young man, then looked at the man's two friends. They had straightened off the bar and were watching the action warily.

"Now, you fellers just better stand easy," Diamond said, "and everybody will get out of here in one piece." Diamond looked at Clint and said, "It strikes me that if I tell this youngster who *you* are, he may decide to leave me alone and try for you."

"Ron . . ." Clint said, warningly. He wasn't exactly in favor of that course of action, but there was no stopping Diamond now.

"This is my friend, Clint Adams," Diamond said. "Now, maybe you want to try him out?"

"Adams?" the man said, wetting his lips. "C-Clint Adams? You mean, the, uh, the . . . Gunsmith?"

"A lot of folks call him that," Diamond said, "but not many to his face. He gets real annoyed."

"Uh, no offense, Mr. Gun—ah, Mr. Adams,'' the man said.

"You mean, now that you know who he is, you don't want to try him?''

"Uh . . . no! No, I don't want to . . . try him,'' the man said, his voice trailing off. "Uh, no . . . that's okay . . . really . . .''

"Can we leave now?'' Diamond asked.

"S-sure, you can leave.''

Diamond looked over at the man's friends, whose hands were held above and away from their guns.

"Let's go, Ron,'' Clint said, and they backed out of the saloon.

"I should be jealous,'' Diamond said as they mounted up and rode out of town.

"About what?'' Clint asked.

"That feller knew who I was and *still* wanted to try me,'' Diamond said, "but as soon as he found out who *you* were, all the fight went out of him. Now, it seems to me I should be jealous of that.''

"No,'' Clint said, coldly, "you shouldn't.''

TWENTY-TWO

Albuquerque was impressive. Its size and its vitality were very impressive to both Clint and Ron Diamond.

"This place is alive," the latter said. "You can feel it in the air."

Clint nodded.

Diamond was worried. Ever since that incident in Los Palos, Clint had been very quiet. Diamond knew he had to apologize to his friend, and he vowed to do so at dinner that night—sincerely, so that there would be no mistake.

"Why don't you turn your reins over to me and I'll take the horses to the livery, while you register at a hotel?" Diamond suggested.

"Sure, why not?" Clint said. "That looks like a likely place."

"Fine with me," Diamond said.

They were looking at a fair-sized hotel with the name "Fairmont" over the entrance. They rode over, and Clint dismounted and handed the reins to Diamond, who said, "I'll see you shortly."

Clint waited until Diamond had ridden away, then he turned and entered the hotel. He knew he was probably being too hard on Diamond for what he felt was a transgression back in Los Palos. Clint had never traded on his reputation in that manner, and it bothered him that Diamond had done it so easily, without even a by-your-leave.

Maybe he was being too hard on his friend. Maybe he'd let him off the hook that night, at dinner. . . .

"Yessir, can I help you?" the clerk asked.

"I'd like two rooms."

"Certainly," the man said, reversing the register book. "How long will you and your friend be staying?"

"That depends," Clint said, signing both his name and Diamond's.

"On what?"

"On how long it takes us to finish our business."

"And what business is that?"

Clint looked up at the clerk and found that everything about the little man suddenly annoyed him: his tone of voice, his little mustache, the way he stood so straight, trying to look taller, and the superior smirk on his face.

"We hunt down and exterminate nosy hotel clerks."

The man's jaw dropped and he stood that way for a moment before trying to regain his composure.

"Yes," he said, "of course. Can I have someone show you to your—"

"Just give me the key to one room," Clint said, "and give the other to my friend when he arrives, which should be momentarily.

"Of course, s-sir," the man said. "H-here's your key."

"Thank you."

Clint went upstairs, wondering if the nosy little clerk would report him to the law for frightening him so.

There was a knock at his door a few minutes later, and he wondered if the clerk *had* talked to the law after all.

When he opened the door, he saw Ron Diamond standing in the hall.

"All settled?" Clint asked.

"Uh, yeah, the horses are being cared for, and I've got my key," Diamond said, looking puzzled.

"You want to come in?" Clint asked.

"Uh, no, I was just wondering . . . What did you say to the clerk downstairs?"

"He was nosy," Clint said, "so I tweaked his nose a little bit."

"He treated me with more respect than I'm used to in a strange hotel."

"That wasn't respect, Ron," Clint said, "that was fear."

"Oh," Diamond said, "I *thought* it looked familiar. Um, do you want to have dinner?"

Clint hesitated just a moment before answering. "Why don't we freshen up first and then meet in the lobby?"

"Sure," Diamond said. "Say an hour?"

"An hour's fine."

There was an awkward moment of silence, and then Diamond said, "Maybe the clerk could suggest someplace decent to eat."

"I wouldn't count on that," Clint said.

"No," Diamond said, "you're probably right. Well, I'll see you in an hour."

Clint nodded and closed the door.

Now he *knew* he was being too hard on Diamond, and he had gone and taken his anger out on the clerk as well.

He was going to have to apologize to Diamond for the way he'd been treating him. After all, Diamond *was* along voluntarily to help Clint with a personal problem, and petty anger had no place in the scheme of things right now, not when he was trying to find out if a friend was alive or dead.

He would definitely apologize to Diamond at dinner, and then they could get on with it.

TWENTY-THREE

Over dinner in the hotel dining room, both men apologized first before getting on with the conversation. Neither was too comfortable doing it, so they did it quickly and got it over with.

"How many newspapers do they have here?" Diamond asked.

"Two," Clint said. "The *Albuquerque Neighbor* and the *Albuquerque Banner*."

"Which is the smallest?"

"The *Neighbor*."

"Give me that one."

Clint stared at Diamond.

"I'll bet I read closer than you."

Clint handed him the *Neighbor* and began to leaf through the *Banner*.

"You know what might be a good idea?" Diamond said.

"What?"

"To try and get some back issues of these papers," Diamond said. "Maybe talk to the editors.

I'll bet anything of interest that happens in New
Mexico shows up in one of these papers. We could
do the same thing in Santa Fe.''

"I could go to Santa Fe," Clint said, looking up
from his paper. "Between Albuquerque and Santa
Fe someone's bound to have heard something.''

"That's a good idea too.''

They both went back to their papers, and then
Diamond looked up and asked, "What do we do
if we come up empty in both places?''

"I don't know," Clint said. "Maybe go to Taos.
Let's cross that bridge when we come to it, okay?
Don't ruin a good idea.''

"Okay.''

"I'll ride to Santa Fe in the morning. How far
could it be?''

The waitress had come over to take their order
and had overheard the question.

"If you'll allow me?" she said.

"Allow you what?" Clint asked, looking up at
her. She was in her late thirties, with brown hair
worn in a bun, full breasts, and wide hips.

"It's about a hundred miles from here to Santa
Fe, depending on where you're going.''

"Thank you," Clint said. "I'll have a steak and
potatoes.''

"And to drink?''

"Can I get a beer?''

"Of course.''

"Beer, then.''

"And you, sir?" she asked Ron.

"I'll have the same.''

"Rolls?''

"Sure," Clint said.

She smiled at them before going to fetch their orders.

"Not bad," Ron said.

"I didn't know you had turned into such a lech," Clint said.

"I'm not a lech."

"Tell that to Marla."

"I told you, that young woman forced her way into my bed!" Diamond protested.

"And there you were, kicking and screaming."

"Just about."

"Well, I'll be heading for Sante Fe in the morning, so I won't be here to see you shame yourself with that comely waitress."

"Ah ha!" Diamond said. "You don't think she's bad either."

Clint changed the subject. "We'll have to find the telegraph office here and stay in touch that way. I'll be in Santa Fe day after tomorrow. You should have something from at least one paper by that time."

"Hopefully."

"If you keep your mind on business," Clint said, as the waitress approached with their rolls.

"Excuse me," Diamond said.

"Yes?"

"We forgot to order coffee," he said. "Could you bring a pot?"

"Of course, sir," she said, giving him a wide smile. "I'll be right back."

Diamond watched her walk away, then noticed Clint watching him.

"Shameless," Clint said.

"Shut up."

After dinner Clint left the dining room ahead of Diamond, who stayed to pay the check. He talked with the waitress while he paid her, then met Clint out in the lobby.

"So?" Clint asked.

"There's a telegraph office just down the street, on this side."

"And?"

"And what?"

"What's her name?"

"Her name is Bonnie," Diamond said, "and she likes older men."

"I'm an older man."

"But I'm older than you."

"Oh," Clint said, "you mean she likes *old* men. Why didn't you just say so?"

Diamond grinned tightly and said, "Let's locate that telegraph office."

"And the newspaper offices," Clint added. "This way you don't have to waste time looking for them tomorrow."

"That's considerate of you."

"Well," Clint said, "I'm just trying to save your *old* legs a few extra steps."

"You worry about your own legs, thank you," Diamond said. "Mine are just fine."

They took a walk and soon located the telegraph office and the offices of the two newspapers, then they repaired to the saloon that was the nearest to their hotel.

Diamond had picked the saloon, saying, "After all, we've got to save *your* old legs some steps."

The saloon was large and busy. There were no tables available, so they stood at the bar and drank a beer each. A couple of the girls came over and made advances, rubbing their bodies against them, but both men declined. Clint never paid for sex, and neither of the women appealed to Diamond.

"They're too young," he said. "I wonder if their fathers know what they do for a living."

"Spoken like a man with a little girl to raise."

"You should see her, Clint," Diamond said, a faraway look coming into his eyes. "She's getting to be so beautiful. She's getting to look like—"

Diamond stopped short, and Clint knew what he was going to say.

"Don't say it," Diamond warned.

"I wasn't going to say anything."

"But you were thinking it."

"Am I wrong?"

"No," Diamond said. "No, damn it. It isn't fair to Lisa to compare her to Delores. Believe me, I don't do it as much as I used to. I really *do* care for Lisa, Clint, and not just as a reminder of Delores."

"I know you do, Ron."

Clint could see now that Ron Diamond—who'd been going by the name Dan Rondo when they'd first met—still had some personal demons to exorcise. Maybe this trip was a way for him to do that. By helping Clint, maybe Diamond was helping himself.

"I've got to get some sleep, Ron," he said,

putting his beer mug down. "I want to make sure I get an early start in the morning."

"I'll turn in too," Diamond said. "I'm not as young as I used to be."

"Me neither," Clint said.

They looked at each other for a moment and then both said, "Want to race?"

TWENTY-FOUR

Clint Adams rode into Santa Fe at noon and left Duke at the livery. Although Santa Fe seemed at least as large as Albuquerque, it didn't have quite the vitality that town had. As a matter of fact, Santa Fe appeared to be downright sleepy by comparison.

Clint walked through the center of Santa Fe, past the stores and restaurants, until he came to a hotel. Inside, he checked in and asked the clerk how many newspapers the town had.

"Two, sir," the man said, "the *Chronicle* and the *Dispatch*."

"Where are the offices?"

The clerk gave him directions, and Clint asked the man to drop his saddlebags off in his room.

"Of course, sir."

"Oh, where's the nearest telegraph office?"

"A block away. Walk out the front door and turn right. You won't be able to miss it."

"Thank you."

Clint left, turned right, and went directly to the

telegraph office. He composed his message to Diamond on the way and told him what hotel he was in.

"Expecting an answer?" the clerk asked.

"Sometime today," Clint said. "Just take it to my hotel and leave it there."

"Sure."

Next Clint went looking for the newspaper offices. He found the office for the *Chronicle* first.

"Help you?" asked the young man operating the press.

"I'd like to see some back newspapers."

"We've got plenty of those," the man said. "What are you looking for?"

"Any stories on Buckskin Frank Leslie," Clint said. "Would you have any?"

"I wouldn't know," the man said. "I operate the press, but I don't read the thing."

"Why not?"

"There are only two types of news in a newspaper," the man said. "Bad and worse. I'll work for a newspaper, but I won't *read* the damn thing."

"That's a pretty cynical outlook for a young man," Clint said.

"I'm not so young," the man said. "I'm thirty years old."

Clint blinked in surprise. He would have guessed the man to be in his early twenties.

"Still, " Clint said, "thirty is not old."

"Are we gonna discuss my age and outlook on life, or do you want to see those newspapers?"

"I want to see the newspapers."

The man led Clint into another room, where newspapers were piled high.

"Help yourself," he said.

"Is there any kind of order?" Clint asked.

"Top to bottom," the man said. "Oldest is on the bottom."

"I'll try not to make a mess."

"Appreciate it."

"Hey," Clint called as the man started to leave.

"What?"

"Are you the editor?"

"Hell, no."

"I didn't think so."

"You want to talk to the editor, you got to come by early in the morning or late in the evening."

"Thanks."

The man waved and went back to his work.

There was a small wooden table and a rickety wooden chair, and Clint made use of both of them as he started going through the newspapers.

He confined himself to the first two pages of each paper. He figured that Buckskin Frank Leslie— alive or dead—deserved that kind of coverage.

He started reading the paper from the day before, intending to work his way back six months. Before he knew it, the pressman had come back in and said, "I got to close up."

"What?" Clint said, looking up and squinting at the man.

"I have to go to dinner," the man said. "You should do the same, but get cleaned up first."

Clint looked down at his hands, which were black with newsprint.

"Don't wipe it on your clothes," the man warned him, just in time, "and you got some on your forehead, too."

"Thanks," Clint said, getting up. "Let me clean up."

"Never mind," the man said. "You can pick up where you left off, either after dinner or tomorrow, whatever you prefer."

"Probably after dinner," Clint said.

"The editor will be here then."

"What's his name?"

The man smiled and said, "Hiram B. Greely—no relation."

"And what's your name?"

"Dobbs," the man said, "Fred."

"Thanks for your help, Mr. Dobbs."

"Call me 'Fred.'"

He walked Clint to the front door and locked it behind them.

"Fred, after I get cleaned up, where's a good place to eat."

"Where are you staying?"

Clint told him the name of the hotel.

"Down the street from you there's a little cafe. It don't look like much, but they can do a steak and fixin's."

"How's the coffee?"

"Strong and hot."

"Sounds good. Thanks again for everything."

Dobbs squinted up at Clint's face and said, "Guess you didn't find what you were looking for, huh?"

"Not yet."

"Gonna try the *Dispatch* after us?"

Clint nodded. "If I don't find what I'm looking for. Are they as good a newspaper as yours?"

Dobbs shrugged and said, "I don't know."

"Oh, that's right," Clint said, "you don't read newspapers."

"Right," Dobbs said. "See you back here later."

"What time do you come back?"

"One of us will open the door at seven."

"And how long do you stay?"

"As long as it takes to put the damned thing to bed," Dobbs said.

He waved as he walked off, and Clint started walking in the opposite direction, toward his hotel. On the way he decided to stop at the telegraph office.

"Did I get an answer?" he asked the clerk.

"Sure did," the man said. "I bring it over to the hotel, like you told me."

"That's good."

"You want another copy?"

"No," Clint said, "I'll read it when I get there. Thanks."

He went back to the hotel, liberated the telegram from the clerk, and took it to his room. He washed his filthy hands in a basin of water, then picked up the telegram again and read it.

C.A.
SUFFERING FROM EYESTRAIN.
HOPE YOU ARE DOING THE SAME.
NOTHING YET.

R.D.

Clint rubbed his tired eyes and knew his friend's eyes must feel even more tired, as he had probably been at it longer.

Also without success.

He slipped into a clean shirt and went looking for that little cafe.

TWENTY-FIVE

Fred Dobbs had been right about the cafe: The steak was good, and the coffee was hot and strong, the way Clint liked it. Feeling refreshed after a good meal, the Gunsmith headed back to the newspaper office. When he came within sight of it, he saw one man being accosted by two on the boardwalk in front of the place. The single man was well dressed, in his fifties, and certainly not in any shape to defend himself against the other two, who were younger and in better shape.

Clint quickened his pace, and as he approached he could hear the words that were passing among the three men.

"... didn't like that piece you ran about him."

"There was nothing legally actionable in that piece," the older man said. "It was well documented."

"Maybe it wasn't legally actionable," the other man said, "but then, we ain't lawyers, are we Cal?"

"No, we ain't," Cal replied, laughing around a toothpick he had in his mouth.

"Excuse me," Clint said.

All three men turned and looked at him. The two younger men looked annoyed, the older man relieved.

"Are you Mr. Greely?" Clint asked the older man.

"That I am, sir," Greely answered. "How can I help you?"

"Could we talk inside, Mr. Greely?"

"Now wait a minute," Cal's friend said. "We got business with Greely, and we ain't finished."

"Have you completed your business with these men, Mr. Greely?" Clint asked.

"Why yes, I have, sir," Greely said. Clint noticed that he was holding a key in his right hand.

"Mr. Greely says that his business with you is finished," Clint said. "Why don't you move on and let me conduct my business."

"Look, mister—" Cal said, turning to face Clint, but the other man put his hand on Cal's arm.

"Let it go, Cal," he said. He looked at Greely and said, "You may be finished with us, but we ain't done with you." The man looked at Clint and added, "Or you either, mister."

"I usually like to know the name of a man who threatens me," Clint said.

"Let's go, Cal," the man said, as he turned and left without introducing himself.

"Shall we go inside?" Greely asked, inserting the key into the lock.

"Sure," Clint said, "let's."

Inside, Greely took off his bowler and fanned his face with it.

"I don't know who you are, sir, but you surely saved me from those two."

"I thought you might need some saving," Clint said.

"And you were right."

"What did they want?"

"They work for Lawrence Penn, a prominent man in town. Apparently he did not like what I printed about him in the paper yesterday."

"Which was?"

"I called him a liar and a thief."

"That certainly sounds legally actionable to me," Clint said.

"Well," said Greely with a smile, "I didn't exactly use those words, but the meaning was clear."

"I see."

"You have the advantage over me, sir," Hiram Greely said.

"My name is Clint Adams."

"What can I do for you, Mr. Adams?"

"I was here earlier, looking at some old newspapers, and I would like to continue."

"But of course," Greely said. "All of our back issues are available to you. Is there something in particular that you are looking for?"

"Anything on Frank Leslie."

"*Buckskin* Frank Leslie?"

"Do you recall something about him?" Clint asked.

"I believe I do," Greely said. "I don't remember

exactly when it was, but I do believe we had something on him in the paper.''

"Can you give me an approximation?" Clint asked. "I've gone back about three months."

"Oh, it would have been further back than that," Greely said. "Were I you, I'd go back about six months and continue back from there."

Well, that would save Clint three months worth of newspapers to go through.

"This thing you ran, it wouldn't have been a story about his death, would it?"

"His death?" Greely repeated. "No, no, I don't think that was it." Greely took off his jacket and started rolling up his sleeves. "You will certainly be here for a while, Mr. Adams. If it should come back to me, I will let you know."

"Thank you, Mr. Greely."

" 'Hiram,' " the man said. "You probably saved me from a beating, you should call me 'Hiram.' "

"All right, Hiram," Clint said, "thanks for the help."

"If you run across it," Greely said, "let me know, will you? You have my curiosity up now."

"If I find it," Clint said, "I'll give a yell."

"Excellent," Greely said. "Now, where is that assistant of mine? We have a paper to get out."

TWENTY-SIX

Clint heard Fred Dobbs come in and exchange some words with Hiram Greely that might have been angry words, except he could tell that they *always* spoke to each other like that. They had the kind of relationship in which neither man wanted to admit how much he liked the other.

Some time later, he became dimly aware of the press running.

Still later, Dobbs stuck his head in the room and asked, "Want some coffee?"

"Sure," Clint said.

He drank it, even though it wasn't very good.

He sat back and began rubbing his hands over his eyes before he realized that he was probably smearing black newsprint all over his face.

He got up and began to look around for a towel or something to wipe himself off with. There was a door in the back wall and he went over to it, not knowing where it led. He opened it and saw that it led outside. He was about to close it when something lifted him off his feet and threw him through the door.

He thought he heard glass breaking.

It was while he was in the air that he thought he heard the explosion.

At least that's the way he reconstructed it later. . . .

TWENTY-SEVEN

When he woke up he was lying on the ground. He sat up and saw that the *Chronicle* office was on fire, burning brightly and hotly because of all the paper that was inside.

He struggled to his feet, aware of the pain in his left leg. He walked around to the front of the building and saw that a bucket brigade had been formed but was doing very little against the blaze.

"What happened?" he asked, but no one answered. He saw a man with a badge standing off to one side and walked over to him.

"What happened?" he asked again.

"Sounded like dynamite to me," the sheriff said. He looked at Clint and noticed that he was disheveled and dirty. "Who are you?"

"My name's Clint Adams. I was inside."

"You were in *there*!" the sheriff asked. "How the hell did you get out?"

"I—I'm not sure," Clint said, trying to remember. "I was standing at the back door, and something . . . threw me out."

"If that's the case you're a very lucky man, Mr. Adams."

"What about Fred Dobbs and Mr. Greely?"

"Far as I know," the lawman said, "they're still in there."

"Did anyone try to get them out?"

"You mean, go in there?" the sheriff asked.

"How long since the blast?" Clint asked.

"Minutes, I'd say," the sheriff said. "The volunteer bucket brigade formed pretty quick. Maybe ten minutes, not too much more."

So then Clint hadn't been unconscious very long.

"They could still be alive in there!" he said.

"Mister," the sheriff said, "maybe you want to run into that building, but I don't."

"Look," Clint began, but just then a woman ran up to the sheriff.

"Dan, where's my uncle?" she demanded.

"Honey, he was inside," the sheriff said. It was later that Clint found out her name was "Honey," and so the sheriff had not been being overly familiar.

"Has anyone gone in to look for him!" she screamed.

"Honey, I can't go in there."

"Damn you!" Clint said.

He ran over to one of the bucket-brigade men and shouted, "Toss some water on me!"

"What?" the man asked.

"Wet me down," Clint said. "I'm going in!"

"You can't go in there!" the sheriff shouted, grabbing Clint's arm.

"You said it yourself, sheriff," Clint said. "I can go in if I want, but you won't." He turned to the man with the bucket and said, "Come on!"

The man shrugged and dumped the contents of his bucket over Clint's head. Drenched, Clint turned and ran toward the building. For one brief moment he was almost repelled by the heat, but he firmed up his resolve and went through the front door.

Although the entire structure was in flames, it was still standing for the most part. There had probably only been a stick or two of dynamite used—enough to do some damage to the interior and start a fire.

He felt the hair on the back of his hands burning, as well as his eyebrows.

"Fred!" he shouted. "Hiram!"

He looked around and shouted some more before he thought he heard someone.

"Hiram!"

"Here!"

He peered through the flames and smoke and saw someone's legs. He rushed to them and found Hiram Greely pinned beneath a beam.

"Where's Fred?" he asked.

"There," Hiram said, jerking his head. Clint looked and saw Fred Dobbs's body, burned beyond recognition.

"The beam that hit him was burning," Hiram said. "This one wasn't."

Clint looked at the far end of the beam and said, "Well, it is now."

Greely looked also and saw that the end of the beam he was lying beneath had caught fire.

"Jesus, get me out of here!"

Clint stood up, grabbed hold of the beam, and heaved upward. It was too heavy for him, but there was no time for him to go back outside and find someone brave—or stupid—enough to go back in with him.

"Hang on!" he told Greely.

He looked around for a stout piece of wood that was not burning. When he found one, he went back and slid it beneath the beam for leverage.

"When I lift it, can you crawl out?"

"You get it up and I'll get out!" Hiram Greely said.

Clint nodded, put his shoulder beneath the piece of lumber, and lifted.

"I'm out!" Greely called, and Clint let the beam fall back down.

He went to Greely, grabbed him under the arms, and hauled him to his feet.

"Which way is out?" Greely asked.

"That way," Clint said.

Greely looked and only saw a wall of flames.

"We'll burn up!"

"When we get outside they'll put us out," Clint said. "It's the only way."

Greely stared at the flames, then said to Clint, "Well, let's get going, boy!"

Clint moved as quickly as he could, taking himself and Greely through the flames. He felt as if his back and arms were on fire, but then they were outside and people were throwing water on them instead of the building.

Before long, both he and Greely were sitting in mud, but they were alive.

They *hurt*, but they were alive.

TWENTY-EIGHT

"The sheriff wants to see you now," the doctor said. His name was Stephen Ives. He was in his thirties, tall and dark haired, and very competent.

Clint sat up and winced as the tape pulled his skin. The doctor had bandaged a couple of spots on his back that were burned slightly and a few more on each of his arms. All told, the doctor felt he was a very lucky man.

"I wouldn't have thought a man could run into that fire and come out with only a few burns. Of course, the hair on your arms and your eyebrows will grow back."

"My skin burns."

"It would," the doctor said. "Being inside that blaze was like sitting out on the desert for a few days, but you'll be all right."

"How is Hiram Greely?"

"He's a little more burned and banged up than you, but he'll recover. He's at home in his own bed, which is where you should be—in your hotel room, I mean.''

Clint got down from the table and winced again.

"My leg hurts."

"I think you might have pulled a muscle when the blast threw you clear. Yes sir, Mr. Adams, you're a very lucky man to have survived both the explosion and the fire."

"Greely and I are both lucky," Clint said. "I'm sorry the same can't be said for Dobbs."

"That's unfortunate," the doctor said, "but I've seen the body. That beam crushed his skull, so he was already dead while his body was burning. We can thank God for that, at least. As I said, the sheriff wants to see you. I can tell him you're not up to it, if you—"

"No, I'll see him," Clint said. "Thanks, Doc."

"Sure. I'll send my bill over to your hotel."

"Fine."

"There's someone else out there to see you as well," the doctor said.

"Oh? Who?"

"Honey Jones."

"Honey . . . Jones?"

"Hiram's niece."

"Oh," Clint said. It was then he realized the sheriff had been calling her by name and not using a term of endearment.

"She wants to thank you for having saved her uncle's life, I guess."

Clint nodded and said, "Thanks again, Doc."

Clint stepped out of the doctor's examination

room and into the outer office, where both Honey Jones and the sheriff were waiting.

"Adams, I want a word with you," the sheriff said.

"What can I do for you, Sheriff?"

"I find it very fortunate that you survived both the explosion *and* the fire."

"So do I, Sheriff."

"Seems to me that kind of luck is . . . rare."

"What the hell are you doing?" Honey Jones demanded before Clint could comment.

"What—" the sheriff started, but she didn't allow him to get any further. She set herself in front of him—between the sheriff and Clint—and planted her hands on her hips.

"Are you insinuating that this man had something to do with the fire?"

"Now, Honey . . ."

"He was *inside* the damned building, you moron, and then after he got out he went *back* in after my uncle—which is more than you did!"

"Honey—"

"I'm taking Mr. Adams home with me, Dan," she said. "You can talk to him after he's had some rest."

"Honey . . ."

She turned her back on him and looked at Clint.

"Would you come home with me, Mr. Adams? My uncle would like to speak to you, and I'd like to see to it that you rest comfortably."

"Well, I'd like that, Miss Jones," Clint said. "Thank you."

"After what you did tonight," she said, "you can call me 'Honey.'"

"Only if you'll call me 'Clint.'"

"All right, Clint," she said. She went to take his arm and came into contact with his burn. "I'm sorry!"

"That's all right," he said. "Shall we go?"

As they walked past the sheriff, Clint smiled and said, "See you tomorrow, Sheriff."

"You can count on it, Adams."

Outside in the street, Clint asked, "What's wrong with him?"

"You humiliated him in front of the whole town," she said.

"I did?"

"He wouldn't go in that building after my uncle, but you did."

"Oh, I see," Clint said. "That's why he's treating me like I had something to do with it."

"Don't pay any attention to him," she said. "Dan Petrie is a fool."

As they walked along the lamplit streets, Clint studied Honey Jones. She had a marvelous profile, now that he had the time to look at her properly. Her nose was straight, her lips full, her chin firm. She had a high forehead and long brown hair that she wore straight back. Another woman might have worn it to hide her forehead, but Honey Jones apparently suffered from no such vanity. She was wearing a man's shirt and a pair of jeans, and she filled out each garment very nicely. In fact, her hips and butt were threatening to bust free, they were so firm and rounded. Luckily, she was tall enough—about five-seven—so that she did not look bottom-heavy.

Clint guessed her age at about twenty-five.

"This is it," she said. They had reached a small, two-story wooden house on a block with other larger houses. "Smallest house on the block," she said, "but it's comfortable."

He followed her to the door; she unlocked it and let him enter ahead of her.

"Where's your uncle?" he asked.

"He's upstairs—asleep, I hope," she said. "Sit down and I'll check on him."

He sat down on a soft sofa and waited until she came back down the steps.

"He's asleep," she said. "Can I get you a drink?"

"Yes, thanks."

"Whiskey?"

"Something cold would be fine."

"I have some lemonade."

"That'll be fine," he said. "I feel like I swallowed some of those flames."

She smiled. "I'll get you a big glass."

True to her word, she came back with a very tall glass filled with lemonade and ice. The glass was sweating, and it felt wonderful in his hand. When he took a sip, he closed his eyes as the coldness of the drink soothed his throat.

"That was a very brave thing you did," she said, sitting next to him on the sofa. She pulled one foot up underneath her.

"I—I suppose it was," he said. "I didn't think about it the time."

"Isn't that the way most brave deeds are done?" she asked. "Without thinking?"

"I imagine so."

"I can't thank you enough for saving my uncle," she said. "He's the only family I have left." She leaned over and kissed him, lingering long enough on his cheek for him to smell her hair.

"Thank you," she said and flushed.

"I'm only sorry I couldn't do anything for Fred."

"Yes," she said, lowering her eyes, "my uncle is very upset about Fred. He was like a son to him."

"I got that impression," Clint said. "I also had the impression that they never talked to each other about the way they felt."

"That's why Uncle Hiram is especially upset," she said. She lowered her eyes for a moment, then looked back up at him. "I'm afraid he's not as free to express his emotions as I am."

She was staring right into Clint's eyes when she said that, and he felt vaguely uncomfortable.

"You'll stay here tonight," she said then.

"I have a hotel room."

"Nonsense," she said. "There's a room down here you can use and a soft bed—softer than any hotel bed. You'll stay here, and that's all there is to it."

"Well, all right," he said. "I am . . . tired."

Suddenly his eyes felt very heavy, and he realized just *how* tired he was—much too tired to argue with her about a soft bed.

"Finish your lemonade," she said, "and I'll fix the bed for you."

When she came back, he had finished the drink and had already begun to doze off on the sofa.

"Come on," she said, helping him up.

He wasn't full awake, so he was only dimly aware of her putting him into bed. He felt her lips on his forehead and, just before he fell asleep, realized that the pillow smelled of her hair.

She had given him her own bed.

TWENTY-NINE

When Clint awoke in the morning, the first thing he realized was that he was naked.

He thought back, very hard, but couldn't remember Honey undressing him. He did remember being put to bed, though, so she *must* have undressed him.

He sat up in bed and looked around. He remembered the smell of her hair on the sheets, and now looking around at the frills in the room, he was certain that she had given up her bed for him.

He was about to toss the sheets back and stand up when she came into the room, moving slowly. When she saw that he was awake, she smiled and abandoned her efforts to keep quiet.

"You're awake," she said. "Good morning."

"Good morning," he said, holding the sheet tightly.

"Don't be shy," she said. "I saw everything you had last night."

"You *did* undress me."

155

"Of course I did," she said. "I couldn't let you go to sleep in those dirty, burned clothes."

"Well . . . I appreciate it."

"Would you like a bath?"

"I'd love one," he said, "but the bandages . . ."

"I'll take care of the bandages," she said. "I'll fix the bath for you. It's down the hall to the right. Here, let me get rid of those bandages."

Her hands were cool and competent as she removed his bandages.

"After your bath, I have some salve to put on your burns, and then I'll bandage them again. I also have some fresh clothes for you."

"Honey, this is all real nice, but—"

"It's less than you deserve, Clint," she said, "believe me. After you're bathed, bandaged, and dressed, I'll have a nice big breakfast for you. All right?"

He stared at her, then shrugged helplessly and said, "All right."

After his bath, Clint pulled on the borrowed pants and found that they fit pretty well, although they were a bit short.

She came into the room then and gently applied some salve to his burns before redressing them.

"Come into the kitchen when you're ready," she said. "I'm taking a tray up to Uncle Hiram."

"I'd like to talk to your uncle when he's up to it," Clint said.

"And he'd like to talk to you," she said. "How about after you've both had breakfast?"

"That's fine."

After she had left, he slipped gingerly into the borrowed shirt, which was a little loose on him. It had belonged to a larger, fuller man, and he wondered who that was.

He looked around for his gun but couldn't locate it, which made him uncomfortable. He hoped the sheriff didn't have it. He couldn't remember if he'd had it on after leaving the doctor's office the night before. First order of business was going to be to find it.

He knew that more evidence would be needed, but he wouldn't be surprised to find that the two men he'd chased away from Hiram Greely that evening had come back and tossed some dynamite through the window. If they *had*, would it have been on the orders of Lawrence Penn?

He aimed to find out.

He knew that the destruction of the newspaper office, the death of Fred Dobbs, and the injury of Hiram Greely were all the sheriff's responsibility, but *he* had been in that building too.

The attempted murder of Clint Adams was *his* business, and he intended to handle it himself.

THIRTY

When Clint entered the kitchen, Honey was already putting breakfast on the table. She had made eggs, flapjacks, potatoes, and bacon. As far as Clint was concerned, she had gone way beyond the call of duty, but that didn't mean he wasn't going to eat her breakfast.

"Sit down," she said. "You can get started. The biscuits will be out any minute. Here, I'll pour you some coffee."

"Honey," Clint said, overwhelmed, "you didn't have to do all of this."

"I would do this and more for you, Clint," she said, standing with her back to the stove. After an awkward silence, she added, "After all, you saved my uncle's life. We owe you everything."

Clint sat down and began to eat. He could tell from the first bite that this would be one of the best meals he had ever eaten.

"Aren't you going to eat?" he asked her.

"As soon as the biscuits are out."

Moments later, she put a basket of piping-hot biscuits on the table, along with some butter, and then she sat opposite him and started to eat.

Clint often wondered if he had missed something by never getting married. Maybe one of the things he'd missed was more breakfasts like this. Still, how many times *could* a wife cook a breakfast like this?"

"How's your uncle this morning?"

"He wants to get out of bed," she said. "I won't let him. After breakfast you can go up and talk to him. He's, uh, got something on his mind that he wants to ask you about."

"Like what?"

"I'll let him tell you."

They ate in silence for a few minutes, and then Clint asked, "What will happen to your uncle's newspaper now?"

"He's going to talk to Sam Wilkens about that," Honey said. "Sam is the editor of the *Dispatch*. Although he and my uncle are competitors, they've always been friends. Uncle Hiram hopes that Sam will let him use his press to put out the *Chronicle*."

"How could two newspapers be put out on the same press?" Clint asked.

"We would use the press during the night, after the *Dispatch* has been put to bed."

"Will Wilkens go for that?"

"I think so," she said, "after my uncle explains everything to him."

"Everything?"

She smiled. "Uncle Hiram will talk to you about *everything* after breakfast."

She was being very mysterious, and for that reason Clint thought he already knew what Greely wanted to talk to him about. It was pretty obvious that Greely would be thinking the same thing Clint was thinking: that Lawrence Penn was behind the explosion.

After breakfast, Clint began to help Honey clear the table.

"I'll do this," she said. "Why don't you go up and talk to Uncle Hiram."

"All right," he said. "The breakfast was wonderful, Honey."

"Thank you," she said. "I don't get much chance to cook anymore."

"What about your uncle?"

"He eats in restaurants and saloons."

"With you here to cook for him, he's a fool."

"Tell him that," she said, smiling. "After you've finished with Uncle Hiram, come back down and have another cup of coffee with me."

"All right," he said. "I'll be right back."

"His room is at the top of the stairs."

Clint left the kitchen, went up the stairs, and found Hiram Greely's room.

"There you are, damn it!" Greely snapped as he entered. "Where the hell have you been?"

"Having breakfast," Clint said. "Honey is a wonderful cook."

"Never mind that," Greely said. "Get me a cigar, will you? Over there on the desk."

There was a small writing desk against a window, and Clint went over and saw the humidor of cigars. He wondered if Greely didn't have enough smoke

in his lungs from last night, but he brought the man
a cigar and lit it for him with a lucifer he found on
the desk.

"Pull up a chair," Greely said, puffing greedily
on the cigar.

"Honey says you want to talk to me about something."

"That's right."

"I think I know what it is."

"You do, eh?"

Clint nodded. "Lawrence Penn."

"That sonofabitch!" Greely said. "He thinks
he's stopped me."

"What's your beef against Penn?"

"He wants to be mayor, but the man's a criminal.
He'll suck Santa Fe dry if he's elected into office,
and I'm not about to see that happen." Greely
hoisted himself up so that he was sitting upright
and could look at Clint.

"I know who you are, Clint."

"You do?"

"Since you first introduced yourself."

"Why didn't you say something?"

"There was no need to . . . then."

"And now there is?"

"Damned right there is," Greely said. "You
were in that building too. You were almost killed,
as well as me. You've got to want revenge as badly
as I do."

Clint thought about poor Fred Dobbs and said,
"Maybe not *as* bad."

"Yes," Greely said, "there is the matter of
Dobbs."

"What about the sheriff?"

Greely shook his head. "He can't do anything. I didn't *see* Penn's men throw that dynamite."

"What *did* you see, Hiram?"

"Nothing," Greely said. "Fred saw them. He shouted and pushed me—probably saved my life. Fred saw who they were, but he can't talk."

"What do you suggest?"

"I suggest that you *make* them talk," Greely said. "Penn will never admit that he ordered it, but the men he hired—the same two you saw last night—they won't stand up against you once they know who you are."

"Ah," Clint said, "you want me to scare it out of them."

"I want you to scare the *life* out of them," Greely said. "Faced with the Gunsmith, they'll testify against Penn and then the sheriff can arrest him."

Clint stared at Greely. He didn't like using his reputation to scare people, but he had to admit it was a good plan. He might even be able to pull it off without anyone getting hurt.

"What do you say?" Greely asked anxiously.

"It might work," Clint said.

"And if you have to kill one of them," Greely said, "all the better."

"No."

"What do you mean, no?" Greely asked. "Those bastards killed Fred. We only need one to testify against Penn."

"I won't kill anyone unless I have to, Hiram," Clint said.

"When did you get so almighty picky about who

you kill? I've written enough editorials on men like you—''

"Men like me?" Clint asked, cutting him off.

"Killers," Greely said. "Men with reputations."

"And you've written articles about *us*?"

"Many times."

"For us or against us?"

"Against, of course," he said. "I don't condone murder . . ." Greely trailed off when he realized what he was saying. "Under normal circumstances, that is."

Clint stood up and stared down at the battered man in the bed. Greely was hurting, inside and out, so he could probably be forgiven for what he was saying.

"I'll see what I can do about finding out who had your office destroyed, Hiram," he said, "and who killed Fred, but I won't kill for you. If you want a man with that kind of reputation, you'll have to keep looking, because I ain't him."

Clint started to leave, but Greely called out, "Hey, Clint—"

"Let it go now, Hiram," Clint said. "Just remember what makes reputations—newspapers!"

Clint stormed down the steps, angry—perhaps angrier than he should have been. He was headed for the front door when Honey called out, "Clint, where are you going?"

He turned and saw her standing in the kitchen doorway.

"I have to go out, Honey."

"You're angry," she said, approaching him. "What did that old fool say to you?"

"Never mind, Honey," he said. "I'll be back to see you later, if that's all right."

"Well, of course it's all right, but what happened?" she asked.

Clint looked up the steps and said, "Ask him." Then he left.

THIRTY-ONE

Clint went directly to the sheriff's office.

"We haven't been introduced, Sheriff," he said, approaching the man seated behind the desk. "My name's Clint Adams."

"I know who you are, Adams," the sheriff said. "My name's Dan Petrie, and I don't appreciate what you did last night."

"You mean, saving a man's life?"

"Grandstand play, that's what it was," Petrie said. "You were lucky to get out alive. By all rights you should be dead."

"Greely and I should both be dead, Sheriff, and that's what I want to talk to you about."

"What are you talking about?"

"I'm talking about two men who work for Lawrence Penn," Clint said. He described them to Petrie and added, "One of them is called 'Cal.'"

"Cal Morris," the sheriff said, "and Johnny Sanders. It sounds like them."

"They were threatening Greely just before the explosion."

"You saw them?"

"I stopped them."

"And you think they did it?"

"I'm almost sure they did it," Clint said. "What I want to find out is if they did it on their own or if they were under orders."

"From who?"

"Penn."

"Mr. Penn's a respectable businessman who's about to run for mayor," Petrie said. "He wouldn't—"

"Why don't we ask him?"

"Who?"

"Us, Petrie," Clint said. "Let's go and ask him."

Clint could see by the look in his eyes that Petrie was afraid of Lawrence Penn.

"I ain't going to accuse Mr. Penn of nothing," he stammered.

"All right," Clint said, "I'll do it myself."

"Adams!" Petrie shouted as Clint headed for the door.

Clint turned and said, "When I get the evidence I need, Sheriff, I'll expect you to act on it."

"Don't you bother Mr. Petrie!"

"If you *don't* act on it, I'll send for a federal marshal."

Petrie swallowed and said, "Now wait. If you do get evidence, of course I'll do my duty."

"That's fine, Petrie," Clint said. "That's all I wanted to hear."

Clint left Petrie's office, sure that he had worked the man into a corner. If he did come up with evidence against Lawrence Penn, Petrie would make the arrest, because if a federal marshal came and found out that he hadn't, he would be out of a job.

Clint stepped down from the boardwalk and realized that he didn't know where Lawrence Penn's office was.

Well, when he found Cal Morris and Johnny Sanders, they could take him there.

Lawrence Penn swiveled his leather chair around so that he could look out his window. From where he sat, he could just make out the charred remnants of what had once been the office of the *Chronicle*.

"Well," he said aloud, "you won't be writing any more about me, Greely, good *or* bad."

And with that he started to laugh.

THIRTY-TWO

Clint walked around town, keeping a sharp eye out for Cal Morris and Johnny Sanders. Along the way he stopped someone and asked for directions to Lawrence Penn's office. He found out that if he had looked up when he left the sheriff's office he would have seen a large, plate-glass window with "PENN & ASSOCIATES" painted on it, and behind that glass would have been seated Lawrence Penn himself.

Clint decided that men like Morris and Sanders would probably be in a saloon, even though it wasn't yet noon, so he started checking the saloons in town.

In the third one he tried, he found Cal Morris, sitting alone at a table. Morris was deep into a bottle of whiskey, without the benefit of a glass. Even as Clint approached his table, the man tipped the bottle up and drained some of it.

"Morris," Clint said.

Cal Morris lowered his bottle and peered up at Clint Adams without recognizing him.

"Remember me?"

"Naw," Morris said. "Do I know you?"

"We met yesterday," Clint said, "although we weren't properly introduced. You were pushing Hiram Greely around, and I stopped you."

"Who's Greely?" the drunken man asked.

"The editor of the *Chronicle*."

"The *Chronicle*?" Morris said. "There ain't no more *Chronicle*."

"Thanks to you and your friend."

"Wha-what friend?"

"Johnny Sanders," Clint said. "Where is he? He was the one with the big mouth yesterday."

"Johnny's the big mouth and the fast gun," Morris said, grinning stupidly.

"And who threw the dynamite?"

"The dyna—that wasn't my idea."

Clint was surprised to get an admission out of the man so easily, but then he *was* drunk.

"Whose idea was it?"

"It was Johnny's idea," Morris said. "I didn't want to have nothing to do with it. I *knew* somebody was going to get killed. I *knew* it."

"Did Johnny know?"

"Sure he knew, but Johnny, he don't care about killin'."

"And you do?"

"I don't like killin'," Morris said, staring at his bottle. "I knew the kid."

"Dobbs?"

"Yeah," Morris said, "Dobbs. I knew him. He wasn't supposed to get hurt."

"Who was, Cal?"

"What'sisname."

"Greely?"

"Yeah, that's him," Morris said. "Greely."

"Why?"

"He was writing bad things about Mr. Penn."

"So Mr. Penn had you blow up the office?"

"No," Morris said, frowning. "I told you that was Johnny's idea."

"And Johnny wasn't told to do it by Mr. Penn?"

"Mr. Penn didn't have nothin' to do with it."

"I'll bet he wasn't so unhappy about it though, was he?" Clint asked.

"Nah," Morris said, "he laughed. He said Johnny did a good job. He said—"

"Cal!"

Clint turned at the sound of the voice and saw Johnny Sanders standing in the doorway.

"Hello, Johnny," Clint said. "Me and Cal here have been talking about you."

"What did you say, you fool?" Johnny demanded of Morris.

Morris looked up at Sanders and said, "I didn't want no part of killin'."

"Shut up, you fool!"

"That's it, Johnny," Clint said. "You and Cal are coming with me."

"Where?"

"To see the sheriff."

"I ain't goin' to see the sheriff," Sanders said. "You think you can take me there, you better try."

"Johnny," Clint said, "my name is Clint Adams, and I was in the *Chronicle* office last night when you blew it up. I didn't appreciate almost being killed."

Sanders's eyes got shifty, as if he were looking around the room for help. Other than Clint and Morris, the only other person there was the bartender, and he was poised to bolt at the first sign of trouble.

"That's too bad," Sanders said, "that you was inside, I mean, but you don't look like you're hurt bad."

"How bad I'm hurt doesn't matter," Clint said. "I don't like somebody trying to kill me."

"We *didn't* try to kill you, Adams," Sanders said. "We didn't even know you were in there."

"Let's go, Johnny."

Sanders held his left hand out to Clint.

"I know who you are, Adams," Sanders said, "but I can't let you take me. Come with me and talk to my boss. He'll make it worth your while to forget all about this."

"Lawrence Penn?"

"That's right," Sanders said. "Mr. Penn's got a lot of money, Adams."

"Morris says Penn didn't order you to blow up the *Chronicle* office. Is that so?"

"Sure," Sanders said, and then he hurriedly added, "but if you want me to say he did, I will. I'll testify that it was Mr. Penn's idea—how's that?"

Clint thought a moment. That would accomplish what Greely wanted, but it wouldn't be right. Although Penn had benefited by the explosion, he hadn't given the order. Clint didn't know Penn, so he didn't know what the man might have been guilty of, but he knew he was innocent in the bombing of the *Chronicle* office and the death of Fred Dobbs, and he wasn't about to railroad an innocent man.

"Forget it, Sanders," Clint said. "I'm taking you and Morris in."

Clint backed up until he was standing next to Morris and then relieved that man of his gun. He didn't think Morris even noticed.

"I'll take your gun," Clint said to Sanders.

Sanders stared at Clint, panic evident on his face.

"They'll hang me," he said. He sounded as if he were short of breath, a sign that he was in a panic. Clint knew that panic could make a man do stupid things.

"Don't panic, Sanders," Clint said, trying to soothe the man. "Just come on over to the sheriff's office with me and we'll talk to the law."

"No!" Sanders said. "No, I can't do that—I can't! They'll hang me for sure!"

"Drop your gun, Sanders," Clint said forcefully. "Don't be a fool."

"I can't let you take me!" Sanders shouted. Then he went for his gun.

The last thing Clint expected was that Sanders would be fast. As the man's hand streaked for his gun, Clint knew he had no time for anything fancy. He drew and fired in one quick motion. The bullet struck Sanders in the center of the chest and propelled him out the batwing doors into the street, where he sprawled in the dirt, dead.

Clint looked down at Morris, who was staring into his bottle. He looked over at the bartender, who was staring at him, wide-eyed in fright.

"I'll need you as a witness, friend," he said to the man.

"Sure, mister," the bartender said, nodding his head. "Anything you say."

"Sure," Clint said, holstering his gun. "Anything I say." He reached down and took hold of Morris by the elbow. "Help me get this man to the sheriff's office."

THIRTY-THREE

Clint could plainly see the relief on the sheriff's face.

"So Mr. Penn wasn't involved?" Petrie asked.

"Not according to what this man told me," Clint said, "and the other man, Sanders. Apparently the dynamite was Sanders's idea, trying to get in good with his boss."

"I told you Mr. Penn was—"

"Mr. Penn was probably very pleased with the outcome," Clint said, "although I believe that relief will be short lived."

"What do you mean?"

"I don't think Hiram Greely's going to take this lying down, Sheriff, do you?"

"What can he do?" Petrie asked. "His paper is gone."

"Is it?" Clint asked. He left the sheriff frowning to himself, with the drunken Morris as his prisoner. Sanders's body was over at the undertaker's.

Clint left the sheriff's office and walked to the Greely home to tell them what had happened.

"Damn it!" Hiram Greely said, slamming his fist down onto his mattress.

"What's wrong, Uncle?" Honey asked. "Clint got the men who killed Fred and hurt you and destroyed the paper. What more do you want?"

"I want Penn!" Greely shouted.

"You're going to have to do that yourself, Hiram," Clint said. "I can't do it for you."

Greely stared at Clint for a few moments, then visibly relaxed.

"All right," he said. "All right, Clint, you're right. That job is mine, and by God, I'll do it. I was wrong in what I said earlier, boy. I thank you for what you've done, but the rest is up to me."

"You'd better get some rest, Uncle Hiram," Honey said.

"I want to talk to Sam," he said.

"Later," she said. "Later I'll get Sam and bring him here."

"He'll help me," Greely said, more to himself than to anyone else. "Sam won't let me down. . . ."

When they were downstairs, Clint said to Honey, "I hope Sam Wilkens doesn't let your uncle down."

"He won't," she said.

"How do you know?"

A sly look came into her lovely eyes as she said, "I've already talked to Sam. He doesn't like Penn any more than my uncle does, and he certainly doesn't like what Penn's men did to my uncle. He's willing to help in any way he can.''

"Well, that's good," Clint said. "Now I can get back to doing what I came here to do."

"Find Buckskin Frank Leslie?" she asked. "My uncle told me."

"Well, I'm trying to find out about him, yes."

"Go and see Sam Wilkens," she said.

"Why?"

She smiled and said, "Just go and see him. I think he can help you."

"Honey—"

"I'll see you later, Clint," she said and went into the kitchen.

He considered following her, then thought better of it.

Sam Wilkens was the one to see.

"You did what?" Clint asked. He wasn't quite sure he had heard the man right.

"I did an interview with Frank Leslie when he rode through," Wilkens said. "I thought some other papers would pick it up, but apparently they didn't. . . . But then I didn't read that stuff about him being dead, either," he added with a shrug.

Sam Wilkens had ink under his nails and a smudge on his nose. As Clint had entered the man was running his own press, and he hadn't been willing to stop until Clint had told him who he was.

"When did you interview Frank?"

"Six months ago."

"Well then, you wouldn't know where he is now, would you?"

Wilkens, a white-haired man about Hiram Greely's age, smiled and said, "I had to send him a
copy of the paper, didn't I?"

"You *know* where he is?"

Sam Wilkens smiled and nodded.

"Will you tell me?"

"Well..." Wilkens said thoughtfully. "Frank
and I got to know each other pretty well while he
was here, which was why he agreed to the interview."

"Well," Clint said reluctantly, "I wouldn't want
you to tell me if you don't feel comfortable about
it."

"He talked about you, you know."

"He did?"

"He said he felt some resentment towards you
while he was still in Arizona."

"And when you interviewed him?"

Wilkens shrugged. "I don't think he himself
even knew how he felt about you."

"Can I see that interview?"

"Sure," Wilkens said. "I've got some copies
around here somewhere."

"Will you tell me where he is, Mr. Wilkens?"

Wilkens studied Clint for a few moments, then
smiled and said, "I might... if you call me
'Sam.'"

THIRTY-FOUR

Late that night there was a knock on Clint's door. He'd been reading the interview Sam Wilkens had done with Frank Leslie and was finding it very interesting. He was finding out things about Leslie he never knew, and he was wondering how he could ever have called himself Frank Leslie's friend.

He had no idea who it could be at the door. Not the telegraph operator: He had already sent Ron Diamond a telegram, telling him where to meet him. Besides, that office would be closed this late at night.

Sheriff Petrie? Had he thought of something to charge him with? Not likely: The man wouldn't have the guts.

Some friend of Sanders? Again, not likely: By now the whole town knew that the Gunsmith was in Santa Fe. The bartender in the saloon had spread that news all over the first chance he got.

Clint decided to stop guessing and answer the

door. He pulled on his pants and padded barefoot and barechested to the door.

It was Honey Jones.

"Honey," he said, stepping back to let her in. "Is anything wrong? How's your uncle?"

"Asleep," she said, closing the door behind her.

"Shouldn't you stay nearby, in case he needs you?"

"I'm here, Clint, because I've decided to take care of my own needs for once."

"Honey—"

"I want you to make love to me," she said, undoing the buttons on her shirt.

"Honey—"

"I know you're leaving in the morning," she said, "and I may never get another chance."

"Honey, if you think you have to do this out of gratitude—"

"Don't be an ass," she said, stripping off her shirt. Her breasts were full and firm, topped by pink nipples that were already distended. "I'm doing it because I want you."

She walked up to him and bumped him with her breasts.

"Tell me you don't want me."

In response, Clint moved his hands to her belt and undid it. He kissed her as he unbuttoned her pants and then helped her out of them.

She did the same for him then, moving to her knees to pull his jeans off. While she was there she bumped her nose up against the head of his swollen penis, then moved her tongue over the length of him. When she took him deep into her mouth, Clint moaned and cupped her head. Her head moved back and forth, her lips and tongue gliding over him slowly, tantalizingly, and he knew that he was in for a long . . . wonderful . . . night. . . .

Honey lifted her marvelously firm butt to him and he took her by the hips, moved his penis up between her solid thighs, and slid inside of her. More and more, he thought, he was finding women who liked sex this way. He wondered if this was the coming thing in man-woman relationships. As good as it felt, he personally liked it better face to face. He enjoyed seeing the look that came over a woman's face when she was riding a man.

Having talked himself into it, he abruptly withdrew himself from her, turned her over, and slid into her that way.

"O God, Clint," she said, "ride me hard! . . . This has to last me a long time. . . ."

He obliged her, gladly.

In the morning the sun streamed in through the window onto Honey's face. Gently, he turned her head so that the sun wouldn't wake her.

He looked down at her and marveled at how young she looked. He had guessed her age at twenty-five, but looking at her now she could have been younger.

He hoped that she and her uncle would be able to build their newspaper up again and properly do battle with Lawrence Penn in their efforts to keep him out of office.

Clint had taken a hand, briefly, in their fight, but

it was *their* fight. In the past he might have stayed to help them, but he had other things to do now.

He had to find a friend, satisfy his curiosity about him, and then get on with his own life.

EPILOGUE

Fairfax, New Mexico, lay approximately half-way between Albuquerque and Sante Fe.

The first thing Clint saw when he rode into Fairfax was the saloon. Above the doors was a sign that said "THE BUCKSKIN SALOON SOUTH." Sitting on a hard-backed chair in front of the saloon was Ron Diamond, who smiled and stood up when he saw Clint.

Clint smiled at the sign and knew he had found Buckskin Frank Leslie.

"Is he inside?" Clint asked, dismounting.

"I haven't gone in," Diamond said. "I figured that honor was yours."

Clint moved to the batwing doors, looked inside, and saw Frank Leslie standing behind the bar. It was early, and there were two men standing at the bar with Leslie, who was listening while the two men did most of the talking. Leslie did that well. It was one of things that made him a fine bartender: He knew how to listen to people.

Clint's guess was that Leslie had traveled around and found out that a reputation wasn't something that he missed. Maybe he felt that he'd made much too big a fool of himself when he left Brightwater, so instead of going back there he'd simply opened another Buckskin Saloon.

Clint reached for the doors, then stopped and turned away.

"We're not going in?" Diamond asked, incredulously.

"I don't think so, Ron."

"Why not?"

"I've found out what I wanted to know," Clint said. "He's obviously alive."

"Yeah, but what about *why* he did what he did? Aren't you curious?"

"Sure I am," Clint said, "but I have my own ideas about why."

"And you're willing to leave it at that?"

"If I walk in there now, I'll be forcing Frank to come up with some kind of explanation. If he harbors any resentment towards me now, walking in there will just make it worse."

"So we just ride out?"

Clint nodded. "We ride out. When Frank Leslie *wants* to explain, he'll get in touch with me."

"And you think he will?"

Clint nodded.

"I don't know when," he said, "but he will."

Watch for

HELLDORADO

**105th novel in the exciting GUNSMITH series
from Jove**

Coming in September!